Souls IN LOVE…
MADLY. TRULY.

BADAL VERMA

INDIA • SINGAPORE • MALAYSIA

Copyright © Badal Verma 2022
All Rights Reserved.

ISBN 979-8-88772-975-6

SOULS IN LOVE… MADLY. TRULY. is dedicated to the fond memories of Varsha, my wife; A misspelled word for life. Varsha is an eternal Sarla (Simplicity) who has soaked me in the rains of love forever. Her aura and era shall continue to embroider her love in the cloudy chasms of my Atarangee Antarman for the rest of my life…

DISCLAIMER

This is a work of fiction. All characters in this book are fictional and imaginary. Any similarity with any person, living or dead, is purely coincidental.

CONTENTS

ACKNOWLEDGEMENTS

Any accomplishment requires the efforts of many people and this book is no different. I thank my wife Varsha whose belief in me inspired, guided, encouraged, and nudged me to start writing and helped me write every day. She had to go with God, and we were separated by that divine dictate. That separation and her love formed the basis of Souls in Love… Madly. Truly. In that sense, this book is more hers than mine.

I also thank my daughters Mishmi and Neetisha who helped me pick up pieces of my life to complete the book.

Many examples, stories, and anecdotes are the result of a collection from various sources, such as newspapers, social media, other speakers, and seminar participants over the past 43 years. Unfortunately, sources were always not noted or available; hence, it became impractical to provide an accurate acknowledgement. Regardless of the source, I wish to express my gratitude to those who may have contributed to this book, even though anonymously.

However, every effort has been made to give credit, where it is due, for the material contained herein.

Thank you all very much.

FOREWORD

"We're all a little weird. And life is a little weird. And when we find someone, whose weirdness is compatible with ours, we join up with them and fall into mutually satisfying weirdness – and call it love – true love."

– Robert Fulghum

Badali, Tu Kuch Aesa Kyun Nahi Likhta Jo Padhne Mein Aasaan Ho Aur Interesting Story Ho …. Har Cheez Ko Complicate Karna Zaruri Hai Kya?!

(Badali, why don't you write something which is effortless to read and has an interesting story … Is it required to complicate everything?!)

While sitting in his study and working on the idea of this book, Papa's thoughts wandered off to what Mumma would often say while sipping her hot cup of chai (tea) and, in moments like these, she would come back to him in the form of a smile on his face. This book embodies my mother…. SOULS IN LOVE … MADLY. TRULY. is Saral Aur Khoobsurat (Simple and Beautiful), just like her.

It is a simple yet riveting love story of Nusrat and Abhay, Saral and Rahul, Varsha and Badal…. It is a story that transcends time and light cones and reiterates the Raabta

(Connection) between two souls, which are eternally betrothed to each other.

Over a span of 192 pages of this book, Papa has weaved a story that celebrates love, life, and relationships. These are things that we often end up taking for granted on our journey to a place that loses meaning if any of these is absent. Only after losing something or someone, do we understand the value of them. But can love ever be lost?

Love is in how someone made you feel beautiful and seen … love is in the dress that they bought you for your birthday …. love is in the last piece of your favourite chocolate cake that they left for you …. Love is in the quilt that they covered you with when you fell asleep at the study table… love is in the tranquil sleep that you got laying your head in their lap… love is in the fragrance of their favourite perfume … While the people may change or leave, the love that they had for you will continue to live on in your heart and memories.

In that sense, love is the only constant in our lives. It is an extremely bewildering emotion … it can make you weak in your knees and yet give you unparalleled strength; it can be shared but has the capability of multiplying manifold in the absence of the beloved.

So read on and immerse yourself in the eternal Varsha (rain) of love, which continues to paint the canvas of our lives … MADLY…TRULY!

– Neetisha Verma

Before We Begin

"I'll be your dream, I'll be your wish, I'll be your fantasy,

I'll be your hope, I'll be your love,
be everything that you need.

I love you more with every breath truly, madly, deeply do,

I'll be strong, I'll be faithful 'cause I'm counting on,

A new beginnin'; A reason for livin';
A deeper meaning, yeah ..."

– Opening lines of Truly Madly Deeply
Song by Savage Garden

Dililah appears to be a deliberately misspelt word for Delilah which means delicate. Delilah, in biblical references, is the love interest of Samson who is famed for his great strength. However, Dililah is the language of the Creator. When God loves some lives a little more, He communes with them through Dililah. Dililah is an imaginary word, and it is an abbreviation for Dreams, Imagination, Love, Intuition, Longing, and Hope. I believe that these words were beyond every interpretation and understanding of life and as such these became the basis of SOULS IN LOVE ... MADLY. TRULY. which is a love story that transcends time.

The story finds its genesis in the Imagination that everything that once lived, lives on forever in the eternity of time. Though our souls must part, time is unripe to know our love story's heart, but hope is very much in sight. Some loves enter our lives and feel destined. But sometimes time whispers … not yet. In this case, we must let go with the faith that if a love is pure and meant to be, it will return. Still, hope shines like a beacon, keeping vigil in the fog of time. And as you grow, that true love may just do the same. Then, the future will find you. When imaginations get the wings, the story is all about a pen going for a walk on paper to meet some conflicts. The conflicts are the essential elements of life and to that extent, the stories are glued together by them, and that comes from some sort of a divide. Otherwise, we'd be in a neutral world with no stories to tell. And there is no greater agony than bearing an untold story inside you.

SOULS IN LOVE … MADLY. TRULY. is a love story of two identical souls who are separated and reunited repeatedly like Cloud and Rain in the eternity of time. The Creator does not permit the memories to cross over the light cones but allows the bonds of love cultivated in the past lives to be carried over to our next lives. Love is sufficient unto love and it enriches the protagonists of this tale when their souls reunite in their next life. The reunion of the identical souls may not happen every time, however, if and when that happens the blessed couples find the SMOTH of Serendipity. The cycle of separations is a must for strengthening the bonds of love and creating the possibility of the reunion of the souls in the subsequent future light cones. The dreams, imagination, love, intuition, longing, and hope constantly refresh the memories of the couples about the bonds of love they carried over from their past lives. The lovers feel the bond, but despite many indications, they do not know why. This is knowing by unknowing. Such bonds of love are above and beyond the concepts of worldly knowledge and wisdom. They do not differentiate between sins and virtues; sufferings and joy; and pains and pleasures. The story of SOULS IN LOVE … MADLY. TRULY. is the story of Abhay and Nusrat who are nurturing the bonds of the love from their past lives, and they reunite with each other in a future life despite all odds. It is a story of the triumph of love, witnessed by Ehad, the time; Awargi, the happiness; and Sajda, the prayer, and narrated by Sukhbir Singh in Qila Nathu Singh, a remote village in Punjab on the Indo-Pak Border.

Abhay and Nusrat are just one couple in love. All lovers are all the same, all the same. Longing to find our way back. Back to One, The only One. In that sense, we are the life itself, and that is our wholeness and fullness that we are here to express and share with ourselves and others and the world. It takes a strong heart to love, but it takes a stronger heart to continue to love after it's been hurt.

Read on …

– Badal Verma

ENCOUNTERS OF SOULS

"Important encounters are planned by the souls before the bodies see each other."

– Paulo Coelho

Sharda and Param

Having spent some happy time with their daughter Nausheen at LA, AVM (Air Vice Marshal) Param Sharma, Veteran Air Warrior, and his beautiful wife Sharda Tanwar returned home to Jaipur. Sharda and Param were a lively couple whose chemistry and companionship were adored and respected by friends and family. The couple was spending a peaceful quality life post the retirement of Param from the Indian Airforce. Their children were well settled. Nausheen was working for Amazon.Com at the US, and Nirbhaya was a fighter pilot of the Indian Airforce who was at present posted at Airforce Station, Ambala.

Atarangee Dreams

Of late Param was seeing a series of strange dreams which were perhaps trying to convey something to him, though that was not making much of sense to him. He would invariably see attractive women and hear strange voices in those dreams. Initially, he let them pass as normal occurrences and did not even remember much, however, a definitive sequence of successive dreams forced him to ponder over some sort of pattern that was being woven in his dreams. Initially, he saw only one woman who would stare and mysteriously smile at him. She was beautiful and her smile was even more beautiful. One day he dared to ask her, "Who are you?"

She smiled and said, "You know me."

When he authentically denied knowing or meeting her earlier, she replied, "Rahul, when my physicality was sublimating into subtlety, I had told you that I would meet you again. How and where I know not."

He did not understand anything and he once again asked, "Who are you? What does all that mean?"

"She replied, "I am a drop of bliss that flows for eons. I am your realisation; experience me with your soul. I can be an attractive woman of your imagination in your external world, but in your Atarangee Antarman (Inner Universe), I am someone more beautiful. You love me for I define your happiness. Perhaps, I have become a figment of your imagination and, maybe, I have spread myself in a mysterious line on your canvas, silently. I keep gazing at you."

Just then the phone alarm rang and he woke up. He forgot most of the dream but remembered her voice which sounded quite familiar, and that she had called him Rahul. "Who is Rahul?", he thought. Thereafter, Param saw such dreams frequently, and he realised that he had known the woman, but he failed to recognise her and he could not fathom Rahul's Raabta (Connection) with him. Dreams continued to visit him and soon the lady in his dream was accompanied by another lady. Yes, the other lady was a dovey-eyed woman with a dusky skin tone and she had some very warm undertone of calmness. She was mysteriously attractive. She wore a peach colour saree layered with symmetrically white lines and a bluish red hi-neck blouse, sleeves of which covered her elbows. Her hairs were open, her eyes were closed and she had turned her neck towards the left as she appeared in his dream. As soon as he saw her, she stated the Master Zhuang's Paradox, "I dreamt I was a butterfly. Now I have woken up and I no longer know if I'm a person who dreamed he's a butterfly or if I'm a butterfly who's dreaming it's a person."

That sudden and random statement puzzled him, but what intrigued him was that he felt he had also met her earlier and heard the same paradox from her. He diligently curbed his curiosity about her and asked, "How is it even relevant to the context?"

She kept smiling and replied, "You had asked exactly the same question even earlier." He looked baffled, but she continued, "That's because you trust that the time is linear. That it proceeds eternally, uniformly. Into infinity. But the distinction between past, present, and future is nothing but an illusion. Yesterday, today, and tomorrow are not consecutive, they are connected in a never-ending cycle. Everything is connected."

Param was realising that the dreams were becoming increasingly complex and somehow, he was able to remember them also. The fear of the unknown was setting up. He shared his thoughts with Sharda and she too felt that the dreams were certainly saying something. But what, they did not know.

True Love Stories Don't Have Endings

In a later dream, Param saw both the ladies looking lovingly at a very cute 10-year-old girl who was playing in her school uniform. The little girl was very beautiful and strangely she had a striking resemblance to Sneha Chitnis, the business baron of their times. He couldn't help but ask, "Who is this beautiful school girl?"

The dusky woman replied, "She is Sarla and everyone calls her Saral. She is Saral."

"And who is Saral?", he asked.

Rather than answering his question directly, she recited a verse…

Falling Through Space and Time

"Falling through space and time,

Towards infinity,

Flying moth in the light,

Just like Saral and you,

Somehow it starts sometimes,

Somewhere in the future.

He did not understand anything and the dream ended. But it left him pondering about that beautiful girl and what those dreams were trying to convey and why.

The Deep Haunting Voice

That particular dream and the face of that beautiful girl repeated themselves several times. Param yet again discussed his dreams with Sharda. After initial denial, they both felt that the sequences of the dreams were definitely indicating a course that was closely connected to their lives. A few days later, he saw the same dream. Everything was the same except that he heard a distant, but the deep haunting voice of a man who was saying, "Abhay, everything is connected. You are existing as Shakti, Rahul, and Param in various light cones and similarly, that little girl is existing as Iqra, Saral, and Sneha. In your present light cone, you are married to Sharda who was the younger sister of Saral, and who died in her childhood in her past light cone. Saral shall meet you again, you won't recognise each other, but the eternal bond will blossom into a love for both of you. Remember, memories are barred from crossing light cones, but there is no such restriction on bonds of souls."

Param had no idea of what was happening, he did not remember most of what that voice told him, and he couldn't understand who was or is Abhay. Who is Rahul? And for that matter, who is Saral? How were they even relevant to his life? What he did remember, however, was that he was holding the hand of Saral and together they seem to be walking in a state of bliss. Suddenly, he saw Sneha Chitnis appear in his thoughts and he felt that she was asking him to come along.

Param did not wake up the next morning; he was no more.

Sharda Misses Param

Sometime later Sharda was in deep thoughts about Param. Her face had a pensive mournfulness and she was scrolling through Param's notes when she saw a Persian poem that he had copied to himself while he was flying the most dangerous mission of his life. The fact that he thought of her while facing the threat to his life should have brought cheers but instead brought tears to her eyes. She imagined someone reading that to her and making her angry with some negative words. But she wanted to read and cry with every sentence, every word….

The Jungle of my Soul

At times I wonder who'll tell you the news of my death.

The moment when you hear of my death, from someone,

I wish I could see your beautiful face,

Shrugging your shoulders, carefree, waving your hands – it's no matter,

Nodding your head, "Wow! He died! How sad!" I wish I could see it,

I ask myself who would believe; Your love burned to ashes …

The jungle of my soul.

Noori Encounter

If we had no eyes then we would be unaware of the existence of colour. What if we are missing an entire aspect of everything simply because we do not have the organ to detect it?

Sukhbir Singh – The Storyteller

The December weather in Punjab is always salubrious. It was raining that day, yet young girls and boys were waiting under the tree to hear another exciting story from Sukhbir Prah Ji (Elder brother). Subedar Major & Honorary Captain Sukhbir Singh was a decorated soldier who post his superannuation, had settled down in his native village Qila Nathu Singh on the Punjab Border. He declined many lucrative re-employment opportunities and chose to do farming after soldiering. He was a happy man and he recently discovered his latent talent in the art of storytelling mainly to motivate school kids of his village school. Every evening he used to narrate tales of courage and valour of the soldiers of the Indian Army to the youngsters of his village. His storytelling sessions were held outdoors in the lap of nature, mostly under a big tree in the centre of the village, or by the side of Namuni Nala, flowing along the border as a manmade tributary of the Ravi River. Sukhbir's sessions, as they were called, were becoming increasingly popular, especially with the local youth. The positive fallout of the same was that the recruitment into the Armed Forces from the village rose tremendously and the local boys and girls started excelling in various sports at the national level. The long-term effect of his talks brought in a sense of discipline and with that, the entire environment of the village changed for the better. Sukhbir's stories about Lieutenant General Abhay Pratap Singh, The Chinar Corps Commander, were very inspirational and popular. Abhay Pratap was the most decorated and hugely respected Army officer in the country who had personally led many daring operations with his unit 10 Para SF (Parachute Regiment Special Forces), an elite commando unit of the Indian Army. Sukhbir was his buddy and together they had undertaken several special missions with humongous success. Interestingly, one of the stories was very special because that encounter had the genesis of Abhay's love.

Noori

Noori was situated in the lap of the higher mountain ranges in North Kashmir. Noori village was perceived to be a prosperous village because of its apple orchards that produced a high yield of high-end export quality apples. It was for this reason that even terror groups left the peace at Noori undisturbed. In Army's threat perception too, the most hostile weather conditions and inhospitable terrain only enhanced its inaccessibility and to that extent, Noori remained a peaceful region. The last recorded operation there was some 23 years ago and that was a botched-up operation that had maligned the fair name and fame of the security forces (SF). However, Abhay held a different point of view. He was reasonably convinced that the inaccessible and difficult terrain as also the prosperity of Noori made it an ideal haven for terrorism. He felt that owing to the proximity of Noori village to POK (Pakistan Occupied Kashmir), and prevailing peace there qualified it to be a hub of activities of the higher rung of terror leadership. Somehow Noori was beckoning Abhay perhaps for a divine design, but the intensity of Counter-Insurgency (CI) operations (Ops) in his company Area of Responsibility (AOR) left no time for him to visit Noori. With the onset of winters, the intensity of CI ops ebbed a bit and Abhay led an area domination mission to area Noori village.

The Area Domination Patrol

The area domination patrol of seven highly trained commandoes to Noori was led by Major Abhay Pratap Singh, Sena Medal himself. From the road head, the patrol climbed up Faiza Mountain towards Noori. As the soldiers reached the higher altitude, the going got tougher, the fog became denser, and the drizzle increased as if to welcome the likely first snowfall of the season. It was a pitched dark night; and dense jungle, deep fog, and rains engulfed every trace of any visibility. Infrared binoculars were rendered ineffective, satellite phones stopped working, and the communication with the base broke down. There was no ambient light and it was so dark that none of the soldiers could even see their own hands. But they owned that darkness and had the intimate knowledge of the ground. Those were the attributes of soldering and the force multipliers that enabled them to always gain an upper hand over the enemy in CI ops. What a marvel of wonder the Army training is! Soldiers were absorbed by the darkness of the night; they were in a state of total disorientation and yet again felt the familiar fear of the unknown that was naturally embedded in such situations. Fortunately, the soothing and steady sound of flowing water in the Nala (Stream of water) approximately 400 metres into the valley below was a reference point as also authentication of their beingness. As per the laid down drill, the patrol secured an area on the obverse side of the mountain and deployed by the clock method for the night. At around 1.00 a. m. the sentry from the Listening Post (LP) reported some sort of noise that was interrupting the sound of flowing water. The patrol was alert and the first instinct was to open fire. They were highly trained commandoes and had encountered such situations in many of their previous operations as well. Abhay managed to hold fire because he knew that fire will not be effective and that would give away their presence as well as position. Even if the soldiers decided to close in, the sound of their movement will not only alert the terrorists, if they were there but also disrupt the listening process. In the given situation, the best option was not to break the listening contact and lie doggo. There was total silence, they could hear the sounds of their beating hearts, breathing, and even of the blood flowing in their bodies. All of them were in the perfect state of meditation and that raised their listening contact to a different level. In contrast to such silence, the sound interfering with the sound of the flowing water was easily discernible as the movement of men and that sound was heading towards Noori. Abhay had carefully read the map and analysed the satellite pictures of the area while planning for the patrol and that helped him link the movement to the single track from the Nala that led to Noori. The training imperatives dictated that patrol moved swiftly, lure the terrorists into the killing ground, block all escape routes, and destroy them with a high volume of intense fire. However, operational imperatives and his soldierly instinct told Abhay to hold on. After an hour, the sound of the movement could not be heard. They waited for another hour before commencing a tactical move towards Noori where name of the game was stealth. In his assessment, Abhay felt that by the time the patrol reached the track, it will be first light and by the time they reached Noori it would be around 10.00 a.m. That was not a worry because sufficient cover of foliage, fog, and rain was always available to conceal their movement. As per his appreciation, they reached the outskirts of Noori by 10.00 a.m.

Beauty of Noori

Unfortunately, the weather at the top was clear, the fog had lifted, and the rains stopped. Chinar cover enhanced the picturesque locale at Noori but failed to provide the patrol cover from observation and/or fire. The positive points were that their binoculars and infrared equipment became operational and communication with the base was restored. Abhay presumed that terrorists if there were any, would be in the village. However, to be sure they needed to observe, work out an operational plan, close in, and take out the terrorists. Accordingly, he made four buddy pairs and placed them in all four cardinal directions for sustained and detailed all-around 360-degree observation. As the buddy pairs took their position in their respective observation posts, they were awestruck by the beauty of Noori. It was like the entire essence of Kashmiriat (Spirit of Kashmir) got compressed in Noori. Picturesque and enchanting, Noori was cradled in lofty green Himalayas and its incredible natural beauty made the village an environmental wonder of peace and serenity. Nature had indeed endowed Noori with implausible beauty, and resplendent with stunning Chinar trees, it looked like a paradise on Earth. The beautiful scenes and the unspoiled nature provided such a mesmerising view of Noori that it almost threatened to hijack the entire process of their observation.

Observation

However, jolting out of the slumber and a state of dreaminess, the observation posts (Ops) got down to their job and prepared detailed written logs of observations. They had to hurry up for they knew that the clear weather was available only for a limited time or maybe for a maximum of two hours. As expected, the weather started packing up and visibility was getting reduced considerably. Night vision devices gave a view of the activities in the deteriorating visibility conditions that had to be integrated with their fair-weather observations and interpreted in a manner to get a coherent view of the emerging situation. The analysis of the observation logs indicated that probably there was a Nikah (Wedding) in the village, accordingly one house was decorated with flowers and it was a hub of a lot of activities. Men were attired in traditional Poots with Mughal type Turbans, headgear, Taranga Belt of Pashmina, and coloured scarf. Women wore colourful Pherans (Traditional Kashmiri dress for women) with heavy embroidery at the neck. The mood was celebratory, soulful music was playing, and there was happiness all around. But the most important intelligence that presented itself was the presence of eight armed militants in the village. The tall terrorist, who appeared to be their leader, was in the house which was perhaps decked up for the Nikah ceremony. The remaining seven terrorists had divided themselves into three pairs and positioned themselves in a manner to provide cover to the leader and protect him should the contingency crop up. Abhay felt that the terrorists had considerably lowered their guards for the prevailing lower threat perception of Noori. The positive outcome of that was they were blissfully unaware of the presence of Indian commandoes in their proximity and to that extent, Abhay's men were able to hold surprise and initiative with them.

The Operational Plan

Having correctly assessed the situation, Abhay was quite clear in his mind that they had to annihilate the terrorists. He was also aware that he did not have the requisite numerical superiority and firepower to neutralise terrorists who were entrenched in a built-up area. Towards that end, he had to quickly decide, devise the method and act swiftly. The easiest method was to storm Noori and kill the terrorists. That was froth with the possibility of collateral damages, mainly the likely killing of innocent villagers in the crossfire. That also meant ruining the happiness of the village and the wedding. The other option was to lure the terrorists into a killing ground at the Nala-Track Junction. That method provided them the element of surprise and also allowed them to utilise the defence potential of the ground of their own choosing to gain numerical and fire superiority over the terrorists. Even the events of the previous botched-up operation were weighing heavily on his mind where a Noori woman and her daughter were raped 23 years ago. A quick appreciation told Abhay to act on the second option. That notwithstanding, and owing to the dense fog that descended on Noori, they had to close in towards the village to maintain the continuity of observation by using the fog cover to their advantage. However, with a view to not getting too close, Abhay asked his team to move a maximum of 300 steps towards Noori. Everything went as per plan except that in searching for a suitable defiladed position Abhay and Sukhbir landed up too close to the house where wedding functions were taking place. They realised that only when they heard the music and the sounds of dancing loud and clear. Abhay quickly decided to pull back. But before he could go back, the tall terrorist came to the first-floor balcony of the house. He was wearing the traditional Poot, but Abhay immediately recognised him to be Rashid Javed. Rashid was a dreaded Lashkar-e-Taiba (LeT) militant and area commander who was one of the most wanted LeT operatives in the world.

The Encounter

In that maddening moment, all the planning and sanity were overshadowed by the basic soldiering instincts and in a reflex action, Abhay fired at Rashid Javed. It was a rare instance of miss when he failed to find the spot between Rashid's eyes in the centre of his forehead, instead, the bullet hit and injured his right shoulder. At that precise moment, she came out and shouted Rashid Bhai (Brother). Abhay just got a glimpse of her beautiful face and yet again he suffered a rare bout of a momentary lapse of concentration while in actual combat. Allah seems to be protecting Rashid. Rashid immediately pushed her inside the room and before Abhay could fire another round, he jumped on him from the first-floor balcony of the house. Sukhbir was stunned by the swift action, he froze and failed to act in time. Abhay's weapon fell with the impact and both Rashid and he started rolling down the slope towards a rocky area to the left of the house and soon vanished into thick fog. Sukhbir couldn't see anything, but he followed the sounds of rolling and action. Unfortunately, he could neither fire, nor influence, nor witness the unarmed close combat between two very strong men. The sound of fire unnerved the remaining terrorists and instead of staying entrenched in their hideouts, they rushed out to protect Rashid. In doing so, they exposed themselves to the accurate fire of the commando teams and six of them were killed instantly. Only the seventh terrorist managed to slip into the thick fog cover. Since there was no cordon, he escaped. And yes, there were collateral damages, one well-dressed and groomed man was killed in the crossfire; and the wedding functions and accompanying happiness came to an abrupt halt.

Unarmed Combat

Concurrently, an epic battle of the titans was raging in the rocky area. Abhay was a 6'3" tall and strong man with a supple and toned body. Rashid was even taller, and he was tough, hefty, and powerful. Abhay had heard many myths about special powers that Rashid possessed and he was testing them in that fight between them. What had angered Abhay was that Rashid had massacred many SF personnel in at least three encounters in the past and Abhay was determined to kill him to avenge their deaths. However, in the current battle, Rashid was having an upper hand. He was holding stones in both hands and was hurting Abhay badly. Rashid had the raw power. As against that, Abhay was physically fit, swift, and a master of the unarmed combat. That was a fight between a radicalised mercenary and a motivated young Army officer. Abhay was fighting to kill or capture Rashid whereas Rashid was more interested in escaping by taking cover of the dense fog. The bulletproof jacket and harness were weighing Abhay down and restricting his movements. Somehow, he managed to get rid of them and attacked Rashid freely. That primitive fight was in a classic contrast to the modern methods of fighting in the age of cyber and drone warfare and it was very savage. In any war, essentially it boils down to one human killing another to survive, only methods of killing are cleaner or dirtier. In the instant case, Rashid had stones in his hands and he was trying to hit Abhay on the head, but Abhay while protecting himself well was hitting Rashid hard, and tiring him down. He surprised Rashid with his innate resilience and strength. However, Rashid was a seasoned fighter, he managed to pierce Abhay's defences and hit him hard in the Solar Plexus. Abhay withered in pain and fell. Rashid picked up a large stone and stood over him to crush his head. Holding the stone high in his hands, he said, "Look at me closely. I am that unfortunate 14 years old boy who saw my mother and elder sister being raped by those bas***ds. They were later tortured, brutalised, killed in cold blood, and their bodies were taken away. Till today their shrieks pierce my ears every moment and don't allow me to sleep."

Humaning of Soldiers

Abhay was in pain, but he felt very bad to learn about the brutality Rashid's mother and sister had to suffer at the hands of some unscrupulous humans. Rashid continued, "My mother wanted me to be a sportsman and win cricket matches for our beloved India, but you guys forced me to become an animal who always prays and acts for the destruction of India." He paused for a moment and said angrily, "Kalma Padh Le." (I am Killing you, remember your God for the last time.) Abhay was all the time thinking of the way to wriggle out of the tough tangle when Rashid was speaking to him. Rashid had perhaps grossly underestimated Abhay's fighting abilities and he had given him more than sufficient reaction time to hit back, and he responded by hitting him very hard on his left shin bone while rolling over to his right. Rashid fell to his left and his head hit a rock and he was temporarily disorientated. Taking advantage of his vulnerability, Abhay pulled out the Indian Army Knife from his shoe pocket, rode his chest, and said, "Allah Miya Ko Yaad Kar Lein", (Remember your God) before slitting his throat. A powerful gush of blood shot out and both of them were drenched in Rashid's blood. Rashid was gasping for air and he spoke with difficulty in broken words, "Don't harm my kid sister. Always protect her. If any harm came her way because of my deeds, God will never forgive you", and he died. Rashid had even taken the name of his younger sister, but Abhay could not understand because his speech was blurred. Abhay was in shock at the sheer brutality of his action. For a moment his tough soldierly exterior broke and he felt some long-buried humanity touch him. Before he fell unconscious, Abhay was thinking that killing a fellow human in such a brutal manner was indeed very stressful even for the toughest of the soldiers.

Follow Up Operations

Abhay having been injured grievously; Subedar Mani Raj Thapa assumed the charge of the patrol. Abhay was shifted to a safer place in the village, Sukhbir was detailed to attend to him, and follow-up operations commenced so that maximum day light hours could be utilised. The searches yielded 7 AK-56 Assault Rifles, 56 Magazines of ammunition, 24 Chinese Hand Grenades, 3 Satellite Phones, US $5000, Rupees7,00,000/-, 7 days of Self-Contained Rations, Maps, and Drone Guidance and Tracking System. All the terrorists were killed, except the one who had escaped. Their identity documents revealed that 5 of them were LeT (Lashkar-e-Taiba) operatives, and 2 were regular soldiers of the Pakistan Army. All of them were Pakistani citizens. More troops were air dashed to sanitise Noori and dispose of the bodies of the terrorists. Village elders of Noori and the family of Rashid Javed pleaded for taking possession of his body, however, that was not agreed to by Army authorities. Abhay was air evacuated to Army Base Hospital, Srinagar.

Khaani

You have to keep breaking your heart until it opens.

– Rumi

Emergency Life-Saving Surgery

As soon as the chopper landed at Srinagar Helipad, Abhay was shifted to the Army ambulance and the vehicle sped away to the Emergency Room of the Army Hospital. Abhay was resuscitated, required blood and other samples were collected, and he was immediately shifted to an ICU (Intensive Care Unit). He was seriously injured; accordingly, he was placed on SI (Seriously Ill) List and his next of kin was informed as per the laid down procedure. Abhay had suffered severe pancreatitis, broken seven of his ribs, and had lacerations, deep cuts, and bruises on his face and upper body. A life-saving emergency pancreatic surgery was performed on him later that night. Several officers and soldiers had gathered at the hospital to donate blood, fortunately, the blood loss was not much, and blood was not required. After the surgical intervention, Abhay was shifted back to ICU and he was heavily sedated.

He regained his consciousness on the third day. When he opened his eyes, he was very happy to see Nalini, Naveli, and Thakur Sahab Bodh Singh Ji Chandel (Thakur Baba) by the bedside. Nalini and Naveli sat on either side of the bed, they held his palms in their hands, placed their cheeks on them and they were crying.

Even the eyes of Thakur Baba were moist when he said, "Beta, In Teen Dino Mein Main Boodha Ho Gaya Hun, Aisa Na Kar Raja, Main Sehan Nahin Kar Paoonga." (Son, I have grown old in these three days. Please don't do this to us, I will not be able to bear such pains.)

Abhay held his tears back with difficulty and put on a brave front when he said, "Don't worry Thakur Baba, you have made me very strong. I am your brave son and God protects me all the time."

Nalini said, "You are very brave, the whole nation is proud of you Bhai."

Naveli informed him, "You have been conferred with Ashok Chakra, Nation's highest civilian gallantry award for your daring action. All of us are very excited to be at the Republic Day Parade (RDP) to see you receive the gallantry award from the President of India. The whole of Niti village wants to be there to see the President pin the medal on your chest."

With the top-class intensive care at the ICU, Abhay recovered miraculously, but he had to stay in ICU for over two months. Thereafter, he was shifted out of ICU to the officers' ward for further care and recovery.

Kashmiri Girl

At the officers' ward, a young Kashmiri girl was deputed to assist the nursing staff in giving medical care to Abhay. She was provided by the hospital-approved agency for giving depth to patient care at the hospital. She had organised every piece of medical equipment well and she was ready to receive Abhay when he was wheeled in from the ICU. As soon as Abhay arrived, she helped the nursing staff in easing him into his hospital bed, adjusted IV (Intra Veinous) drips and other tubes smiled, and said, "Good evening, Sir, I am Hala Khan, and I will be your care giver here. You will get well very soon" All Kashmiri girls are pretty, but Hala was exceptionally beautiful. Everyone in the hospital was fascinated by her charm and innocence. She was very affectionate and sincere about doing her job. She had an extra sparkle in her eyes, she was efficient in her work, and she was soft-spoken. Surprisingly, even her accent did not have the heavy undertone of the Kashmiri language. With her dedicated care, and helping nature, she won the hearts and trust of everyone in the hospital. Soon, she became a friend of Nalini and Naveli, and even Thakur Baba treated her like his third daughter. After about another week or so when Abhay's condition was stable, Thakur Baba, Nalini, and Naveli returned home. As his condition continued to improve further, Hala had taken upon herself the responsibility of the complete nursing care of Abhay. She always remained positive and encouraged him to have faith in himself for a complete and early recovery. Her efforts bore fruits and accelerated the process of his healing. As the familiarity between them grew, she called him by his maiden name instead of Major Abhay Sir. And in recognition of her devotion to duty, Abhay called her Khaani. She loved her new name and so did everyone else as she became Khaani for everyone. She kept in touch with Nalini and regularly updated her about Abhay's condition.

Are Terrorists Your Enemy

The staff in the hospital saw her deliberately coming close to him. She would strike up a conversation with him on various subjects. Many Army officers, their wives, and soldiers visited Abhay, and Khaani was deeply impressed to observe the bonding and the intimacy of soldiering. One day she asked him, "What is the significance of the formation sign that all Army men wore on their left arms?"

"Formation signs are symbols of the identification of their Army formations", he replied.

"I saw one in which a hand was holding a dagger. What does that mean?"

"It means, 'Hold Fast, Thrust Deep' into the chest of your enemies."

"Are Pakistani soldiers your enemy?"

Abhay's reply unnerved her when he said, "No, they are not."

"Are terrorists your enemy?"

He knew what she was aiming at and he once again replied, "No."

"Why do you all kill them, then?"

"See Khaani, no soldier is an enemy of any soldier. All soldiers dedicate their services to their nation, they obey orders and perform their duty. They kill because if they don't kill, they would be killed. For the same reason, we kill the terrorists."

"But terrorists are not soldiers, then why do you kill them?"

"We kill them only when they raise weapons against the state and kill soldiers as well as innocent civilians." Having said that he asked, "Why do you think terrorists kill defenceless civilians?"

Soldierly Instincts

Khaani looked a bit confused and as she began to say something, a team of doctors walked in and informed Abhay that he was fit to be discharged and sent on six weeks of sick leave. They further said, "Your family has requested Ms. Hala Khan to accompany you for the continuity of your care at home. She has agreed to do so, and tendered her resignation to the agency accordingly." Abhay looked at Khaani with gratitude, she just smiled and said nothing. Abhay was happy. He felt a kind of bond with Khaani that pulled him towards her. There was something in her face that made him feel that he had known her earlier, but he was unable to remember when and where. He saw affection in her sparkling eyes, but what perturbed him was that he also noticed a kind of indifference in them at times, and that alternated with her affection most of the time. He attributed her stance to the medical ethics that mandated that the caregivers could not get emotionally involved with their patients while giving care as a possible reason for her to maintain a dignified distance from him. His feelings for her were real. He knew he was in denial, but he was attracted to her. His soldierly instincts were, however, sensing danger, and whenever he felt that way, it so happened that he saw pure affection in her eyes at the same time. She was an innocent girl and he couldn't understand her affection beyond the imperatives of the medical care, and he felt there was nothing more than that from her side. He had spoken to himself many times in the past, "Why are humans so complex? Rahen Toh Sabhi Seedhi Hain, Mod Toh Saare Man Ke Hain." (Ways of life are simple, complications are of our hearts.) At times, however, he felt that Khaani was deliberately trying to come closer to him. Her care was not purely professional, and sometimes it tended to become somewhat personal. The warmth of her being so close to him stirred his raw emotions. That bouquet of mixed signals from her was inciting the soldierly instinct that told him to tread carefully. But what intrigued him more was his attraction towards her for sure.

Suspicion

But Sukhbir did not think that way. To him, many of Khaani's activities looked suspicious. He noticed that on receiving a particular call, she would leave all work and rush to a secluded corner to have a long conversation. Sukhbir could not hear such conversation, but he would observe that Khaani always looked a bit disturbed after such calls. She would be worried and wouldn't even go to Abhay for a considerable time after those calls. She would also overtly become very protective of Abhay whenever Hania Saeed and Sana Khan of her agency came to see him in the officers' ward. She had to accompany them when they went back and mostly returned with some confusing expressions on her face after meeting them. Sukhbir was quite certain that those actions were connected, but he was missing the point. He thought of sharing his observations with Abhay but stopped short of it fearing those may hamper the process of his expeditious healing. He was Abhay's buddy and he had to protect Abhay at all costs. He knew that Abhay had a very sharp sense of soldierly instincts and that combined with his reflex actions gave him special powers to ward off all dangers coming his way. But Khaani was perhaps playing on emotional turf, and that space was unknown to Abhay. Abhay was a novice in the fields of feelings, and Khaani could be very dangerous out there. Abhay was a hero in real life and a national asset. Sukhbir had to be very careful, keep a discrete watch on every action of Khaani, and be there for Abhay all the time.

The Land of Gods

Finally, the day arrived when Abhay was found fit to be discharged. Discharge formalities having been completed, Abhay was granted six weeks of sick leave, and he was shifted to a guestroom in Badami Bagh Cantonment for the night. The next day, Abhay, along with Sukhbir and Khaani took an Indigo Flight to Delhi and the connecting flight from Delhi to Dehradun on the same day. Both Nalini and Naveli were there at Jolly Grant International Airport to receive them. They moved in two cars to the outskirts of Mussoorie where the family had their palatial bungalow sprawling over ten acres of green land. The view of the place was mesmerising. When seen from there, the meandering meadows, bubbling creeks, the dense woods of deodar, and the Himalayan peaks offered a panoramic view of the landscape. Khaani had a kaleidoscopic view of "The Land of Gods" and that gave her a familiar feeling of being in her native land of beauty. Abhay's room presented a phenomenal view of nature and Khaani was accommodated in an adjacent room. With the loving care of Khaani and the affection of Nalini and Naveli, Abhay recovered miraculously. The three girls became good friends and the home was filled with the happiness of their abundant laughter and playfulness. Nalini and Naveli had completed their graduation from Lady Shriram College for Women and Khaani did hers from Saint Stephen's College in the same year. They recounted having a lot of fun at various college fests on both the North and South campuses. Khaani became a daughter of the home and even Thakur Baba was very fond of her. Sukhbir did not let his guard down, he constantly observed whether there were any suspicious activities around Khaani, and kept a strict vigil to protect Abhay against all threats.

INVISIBLE BONDS

Listen to your soul.
It's older than your heart and wiser than your mind.

The Glimpse of The Fourth Lady

Khaani spent most of her time with Abhay. They went for walks together and soaked themselves amply in the benevolence of Nature. Khaani had a reasonably good knowledge of Nature, she could identify various species of birds, and she knew about jungle herbs. Abhay was coming close to her and she knew it. His affection and attention were disturbing her. She felt a special kind of bond with him that she had not experienced with anyone else earlier. She somehow thought she had an idea of some man she would fall in love with. However, that feeling for him was a kind of déjà vu. She was falling in love with him, but she knew she could not afford to do that. Abhay thought a lot about their emerging relationship and he somehow traced the connection to the strange dreams he was having since his childhood where he saw and remembered three women clearly. However, he always had a glimpse of the fourth and did not remember her. The ladies of his dreams were exceptionally beautiful. One of them had a dusky skin tone, the second was always naughty, and the third was simply beautiful. All of them were always smiling in his dreams while pointing towards the fourth one who was the most beautiful girl amongst all of them. But why were the three ladies constantly drawing his attention to the fourth girl? Did he see the glimpse of the fourth lady at Noori on the day of the encounter? He wanted to brush that thought aside, but he could not because he felt that Khaani perhaps resembled the fourth lady of his dreams. Was he seeing her in his dreams? Why should he? And what if those dreams were for and about Khaani? But he was seeing those dreams much before he had even met her. He was not even sure of his feelings for her. He most certainly had no idea if that could be love, but for sure he felt uniquely happy whenever she was with him. He wanted to tell her that but could not muster enough courage to do so.

Expression of Love

It was a very pleasant coincidence that he saw the dream that night in which he expressed his love to someone whose face he could not recollect, but remembered the exact conversation. He also saw the dusky beauty and remembered their conversation in the dream. He felt the entire sequence had repeated itself somewhere in his past. The dream unfolded…

"Do you love me?", she asked unexpectedly, but deliberately.

He was not prepared for that and as if in a reflex response he replied, "Of course, yes, and I love you very much. Eighteen thousand times worth."

"How do you know that?", she appeared to be having fun with his awkwardness.

However, he was serious about finding words for the expression of his love, "Love is no voice, nor any spoken words. It is only silence that does speak to hearts and loving hearts hear that too. It does not pause nor stop and never extinguish. Just a drop of celestial light flowing from eternity. It is only a feeling and I do feel it within the depth of my soul. If that is the love, I feel it whenever I am with you. When your eyes are lit up with a smile and the halos of light entwine your bedazzled lashes, your lips tremble, but don't say much as if trying to hold onto many silent untold tales, I sense my love. Love is as it ought to be, it is complete that way. I have seen the twinkling fragrance of love in your deep eyes. I am blessed to be touched by the love and fortunate enough to have solemnised our union into a worldly relationship as well."

Who was She?

Just then the dusky beauty gate crashed his dream and asked, "What if everything that came from the past was influenced by the future?" That thoroughly confused him. Without even bothering to look at him, she continued, "The spinning wheel turns, round and round in a circle. One fate is tied to the next. The thread, red like blood, cleaves together all our deeds. One cannot unravel the knots. But they can be severed. Someone severed yours, with a sharp blade. Yet something remains behind that cannot be severed. An invisible bond!" Suddenly he felt he was shot in his right shoulder and he woke up abruptly. He immediately checked his shoulder and found that to be alright. However, he realised that a lot of thoughts were cluttering his mind space and they were asking so many questions. Questions like, "Who was she? Were they in love? Was he married to her? When? Where? Why couldn't he remember her face? What was severed with the sharp blade? Were those knots a metaphor for someone's life? Who died? What was the significance of the unsevered invisible bond? Were the invisible bonds the reason for the love you feel for someone? Where do the bonds originate and why? Do the souls meet somewhere before bodies find each other elsewhere?"

Maggie Point

Abhay came out of the tangle of his thoughts when Khaani came to escort him to his morning walk and mild exercises. As they came out to the beautiful countryside, a drizzle greeted them and a mild breeze caressed their faces. Though there was a nip in the air, they continued to walk and grasp the beauty and benevolence of Nature in their beingness. When they had walked some two km or so, drizzle intensified, and clouds descended to the ground and engulfed the young man and woman into them. Accidentally, Khaani's hand touched Abhay's hand and he felt a hitherto unknown joy traversing through his body. Perhaps Nature too was having fun, rains intensified and the couple took cover under a shed near Maggie Point. Khaani settled Abhay and fetched two hot glasses of tea. Abhay told Khanni, "I want to know you a little more. Tell me something about you." For whatever reason, Khaani was not comfortable and Abhay did notice her sense of uneasiness about his question. However, she replied, "I am a simple girl and I hardly have anything to say about me." Abhay made her feel comfortable but persisted with his desire to know more about her. She said, "I was born at Rahimabad, approximately 20-25 km from Srinagar. My father was an art teacher at the Government school in Srinagar and I completed my schooling at the same school. I scored good marks and did my graduation course in English literature from Saint Stephen's College, Delhi. Thereafter, I moved to the Breach Candy Hospital, Mumbai where my Maamu (Maternal Uncle) was working as a lab technician. I did a short course there in nursing care. I stayed in Mumbai for six months and came back to Rahimabad when my Ammi (Mother) fell ill. That's all that is about my petty uncomplicated life." She almost heaved a sigh of relief when her story was over in less than five minutes. Abhay noticed that sense of relief, she realised that and they both laughed. But Abhay definitely felt there was much more to her that she did not want to reveal. That was his gut feeling and he always trusted his instincts. But what would be holding her back? Were Sukhbir's observations, correct? Who is Khaani and why should she tell lies? Why did she make up her story? Abhay felt that a steady flow of thoughts was clogging his mind space.

Every Life is a Special Story

He thought, "We just become the prisoners of these intense thoughts and emotions along with our fragile egos and narcissistic injuries. That makes our mind a mentor and masterpiece of storytelling of rupture and repair of our relationships with the world. Every life is a special story of its own. It is special because it cannot be completed till one dies, and one writes one's own story as a dictation from the unknown who is the reason for individual imaginations to assign the quality to one's story. One's story is the perfect form of a narrative of a life. Some stories are artful, beguiling, dangerous, or delightful narratives; they contain a diverting amount of energy. Within an hour, a whole world, its inhabitants, and its often-vexing propositions can be consumed. And a disquieting tale brings a lot of perspectives. These stories can deal so effectively with dark matter. The best stories are like suitcase nuclear devices – small, disproportionately powerful, capable of demolishing normality and morality with exceptional fineness. We may agree to disagree, but everyone has a story, made up of several chosen stories, that we repeatedly tell ourselves about ourselves, and tell others too; it hinges on how we want to be seen. The narrative plays a role not only in shaping our self-concept but also in how we approach situations, relationships, and decision-making. One's composite personal story contains events or aspects of our history which may be factual, but the way we select some and leave others out, subjectively interpret them, and thread them into our main personal narrative to reshape, and alter the bare facts. How we feel about our lives right now is a matter of stories that we tell ourselves repeatedly. What are these stories? How do you make sense of who you are? Doesn't your composite personal story paint you primarily as victor or victim, popular or lonely, successful or unsuccessful? One may realise that none of these on their own can be wholly true. Yet for many, these one-sided stories repeated over time can become so distorted and damaging that they hamper their ability to live balanced, happy lives. Rebecca Solnit writes: "We think we tell stories, but stories often tell us; tell us to love or hate, to see or be seen. Often, too often, stories saddle us, ride us, whip us onward, tell us what to do, and we do it without questioning." Khaani noticed that Abhay was quiet for some time and she felt for the first time in so many days that Abhay probably did not believe her story. She looked a bit worried and even that expression did not go unnoticed by Abhay. She had to make Abhay talk to shift his attention away from her, but before she could do that Abhay suddenly asked, "Have you been to Dehradun earlier?"

Khaani was taken aback, and even hesitated, but she said "No." Having answered his question, she quickly changed the topic and said, "Your family is very affectionate and cultured."

Not My Blood Family

"Yes, they are excellent humans, but they are not my original family." Abhay had never shared that with anyone but he felt quite comfortable sharing with her.

She had never seen anyone love the way Thakur Baba, Nalini, and Naveli loved Abhay. She could not believe what Abhay had just said and she immediately asked, "What do you mean? Are you in your senses? Aren't you telling a lie Abhay?

"I never lie. That's true. They are not my original family. But they are the ones who are my entire universe. I live because they love me so much. I have never loved anyone more than them." Then he said something which startled her. He said, "Now I love you as much, and all of them love you a lot."

As he said so, there was a loud thundering in the sky, and a scared Khaani clung to Abhay in a reflex action. She moved away as quickly as she came close to him, and while trying to manage her breath, she said, "Abhay, heavy rains are coming, let's rush back home. It is almost breakfast time and I have to give you the medicines also." For the entire duration of their walk back, Khaani hardly spoke. She was still stuck in the way she felt when she embraced him in those beautiful moments of her life that rainy morning. She could be fighting her feelings, but Abhay did not think much. He was happy to accept his love. Later that afternoon, Khaani brought coffee for him and sat down with him on the balcony of his room. It had poured heavily through the afternoon, and a slight drizzle was continuing. All the trees, plants, and flowers were washed by the rains and the entire landscape presented a fresher version of itself. They were enjoying nature as also their coffee. Both of them were unusually quiet. Suddenly, Khaani said, "Abhay, I am quite surprised that Thakur Baba, Nalini, and Naveli are not your family."

"No, they are my family. I love them, and they love me more."

"But?"

"I meant they aren't my blood family."

"Can you please share with me the story of your life?"

Abhay Pratap Singh

"Men are born soft and supple; dead they are stiff and hard. Plants are born tender and pliant; dead, they are brittle and dry. Thus, whoever is stiff and inflexible is a disciple of death. Whoever is soft and yielding is a disciple of life ... The soft and supple will prevail."

– Lao Tzu

Happy Family

Abhay began by telling her, that the story of his life was quite interesting and that she would enjoy listening to that. Abhay's story started playing in his mind, he saw his life as a movie and he commenced the narration of the same to her. He was born in a poor household in the village of Nangal Raya, near Delhi Cantonment (Cantt) Railway Station. Om Singh, his father was working at the Central Ordnance Depot (COD), Delhi Cantt. His mother Kamala Devi loved him a lot and she was grooming him well to be a good human being. She played with him, fed him well, sang Lories (Lullaby) to him, told bedside stories and she would take him along whenever and wherever she went. She treated him like her prince and was fiercely protective of him. She had drilled into him three things that he followed to date. These were, respect women, always speak the truth, and always smile at your difficulties. As far as Abhay was concerned, she was his entire universe. His father was a good and happy-go-lucky man. He would always find time to take him out on his bicycle and show him around the countryside. He would take his wife and son for eating out and/or watching a movie every Sunday. He remembered his mother used to sit on the carrier and he would sit on a small seat fitted to the front frame of his father's Raleigh Cycle. Theirs was a poor, but blissful family. Unfortunately, he lost his mother when he was just two-year-old. Their entire world came crashing down. His father tried his best to take care of him to the best of his capability, but his best was nowhere close to the normal care of his mother. He loved him, but he had to go for his job also.

Radha and Swarn

Radha Kaki (Auntie) was their neighbour and she was his mother's best friend. She took over the responsibility to look after Abhay when his father went to work. She did not have a child of her own. She loved him like her son and she always encouraged him to smile at his difficulties. He missed his mother and even cried a lot, but as a child, he was in the blessings of God who helped him bear the loss of his mother reasonably well and gave him a feeling that she watched him from above. He was a naturally gifted child and the whole village loved him. He was baptised by the darker side of life at a very tender age. Under extreme societal pressure, his father remarried mainly to find a mother for his son. His new mother Sheela Devi was good. She treated him well. However, she did not like his closeness with Radha Kaki. In due course of time, his new mother was blessed with twin daughters, Shruti and Surbhi when he was just four-year-old. Thereon, his parents did not have time for him. He felt like an orphan and that pushed him even closer to Radha Kaki. Seeing him survive like that broke her heart and the only remedy she found was she loved him even more. She knew he was not hers, but she connected with him emotionally and she cared for him like he was her child. Swarn Kaka (Uncle), Radha Chachi's husband, was a cobbler and he went to New Delhi Railway Station every day to work and earn their livelihood. Then came the fateful day in Abhay's life when destiny decided to rewrite his story of life.

Smile in Difficulty

The day began, as usual, and a hungry him was sneaking out to Radha Kaki's home for a Roti (Indian Bread). As he passed by his mother's room, he saw her sleeping soundly and one of his twin sisters was almost falling from the bed. He ran and caught her, but in doing so, he also fell with his stepsister on his chest. That woke up Sheela Maa, she picked up her daughter, and an overprotective mother in a gross misunderstanding that he was trying to harm her kid, delivered a tight slap on his left cheek. That was the first slap of his life. Surprisingly, he did not cry and as he moved out of the room, he saw his father rushing into the room and he did not even look at him. The way his loving father ignored him brought tears to his eyes. That triggered the first thought in his young broken heart to run away from his loving home and God heard him. Abhay came out crying, he felt Kamala come to him, held his soft hand, led him to Radha's home, and handed him over to her. He looked up towards the sky and felt his mother telling him,

"Abhay don't, don't cry son." He remembered that she always wanted him to smile at his difficulties. He wanted to cry, but he did not cry. Suppressing his tears, he tried to smile, and the resultant expression on his face was so formed that it could make anyone cry. Radha Kaki cried, she did not ask him anything, she didn't need to as the fingerprints on his tender cheek had leaked the story of that morning. She gave him a Roti to eat, but that day he refused to eat. Perhaps, he was angry. Life was teaching him life, the hard way. To distract him from his agony, Swarn Kaka took him along with him to New Delhi Railway Station on that day.

You Dropped the Photo

That was an unusually busy day for Kaka. Abhay watched him keenly as he polished shoes and repaired Chappals (Sandals and Slippers) the whole day. When it was time for them to wind up, a tall aristocratic man wearing expensive clothes and Garhwali Brahma Kamal Topi (Traditional Cap of the Indian state of Uttarakhand) stopped at their corner. He wore a gold watch on his jacket, the gold chain of which slung across his chest. His well-polished shoes were soiled and he wanted Swarn Kaka to clean the same for him. Kaka cleaned his shoes and he gave him a hundred rupee note in return and asked him to keep the change; that was much more than the rate normally charged for polishing the shoes. The man glanced at little Abhay, he thought for a moment, drew his wallet out once again, gave Rs 50/- to him, and thereafter he immediately walked away. Abhay noticed that the kind man had dropped something from his wallet while he was drawing the money out to give it to him. He looked at Swarn Kaka who told him to run and return the same to him. There was a big rush on the platform, the man moved swiftly in long strides, and Abhay literally ran to catch up with him, but he missed him. Abhay kept moving in the direction in which the man was going, but he could not see him. He was lost and as he decided to turn back, he saw the man boarding the train. He ran and boarded the same compartment. He looked for the man, and he was nowhere to be seen. He did not even realise that the train had started moving slowly. He was disappointed, just then he saw the man peep out of a coupe. He rushed to the coupe and reached there before he could close the gate of the coupe. The gentleman was quite surprised to see Abhay standing before him. He looked quite irritated when he disdainfully asked, "What are you doing here and in this compartment?"

Abhay just extended his hand and said, "Saheb Ji Aapne Ye Photo Gira Di Thi Ji. Wahi Lautane Aaya Hun Ji." (Sir, you had dropped this photo. I have just come to return that to you.)

The Destiny Took Over

As soon as the man saw that photo, the frown on his face gave way to an expression of affection and gratitude, and he got Abhay inside his First Class AC Coupe. The photo was of Thakuraien Sahiba Sangeeta Devi Ji, his wife whom he had lost recently to Glioblastoma (Brain Cancer). She was just 31-year-old. She was a very beautiful, elegant, and graceful lady whom he loved very much. By that time, the train had picked up speed and the man did not know what to do with that innocent boy. He toyed with the idea of pulling the chain and dropping it immediately for even if the train stopped, he could not leave the 4-year-old child on the rail tracks unattended at night. There was something about Abhay and as if guided by the dictate of some divine ordain, the man felt his affection flow towards him. He asked the boy to sit and gave him water and some biscuits to eat. Abhay had water and finished off all the biscuits almost immediately. He was hungry. He had only a slap and nothing else since morning that day. But he kept standing in a corner. The man again asked him to relax and sit down. Abhay was intimidated by the luxury of the coupe and he sat down on the floor. He asked him to sit on the berth. At the dinner time, Abhay got the normal dinner that the Indian Railways serve, but that was the best meal of his life that his family could never afford. As soon as he finished his food, he slept off. The man saw him snug into himself as he felt cold in the AC coupe. He covered him with a blanket and the boy slept peacefully, unmindful of what the future had in store for him. Thakur Saheb eased into his night comforter and took out "The Prophet", a Khalil Gibran book, to read before he slept. It was a coincidence of sort that the page he opened was about Gibran's interesting take on children. Abhay spoke in his sleep, and he was perhaps talking to his Kamala Maa. Thakur Saheb read, "And a woman who held a babe against her bosom said "Speak to us of Children" ... And he said,

Your Children Are Not Your Children

"Your children are not your children,

They are the sons and daughters of life's longing for itself,

They come through you but not from you,

And though they are with you yet they belong not to you.

You may give them your love but not your thoughts,

For they have their own thoughts,

You may house their bodies but not their souls,

For their souls dwell in the house of tomorrow.

Which you cannot visit, not even in your dreams,

You may strive to be like them,

But seek not to make them like you,

For life goes not backward, nor terries with yesterday.

You are the bows from which your children

As living arrows are sent forth,

The archer sees the mark upon the path of the infinite,

And he bends you with his might.

That his arrow may go swift and far,

Let your bending in the archer's hand be for gladness,

For even as he loves the arrow that flies,

So, he loves also the bow that is stable."

He looked at the innocent face of Abhay and saw a life longing for itself. He decided that the boy will come with him, come what may.

Abhay was Missing

When Abhay did not return after a reasonable amount of time, Swarn got worried, and he started looking for him frenetically. After being exhausted completely, at around 10.00 p.m. that night, he informed the railway police and lodged a missing report with them. Swarn was crying and he was even worried about the fact that Abhay had not eaten anything since morning that day. Radha was waiting for them and when they did not return much beyond the usual time of their arrival, she was worried about both Swarn and Abhay, more about Abhay. Surprisingly, there was no such concern or worry for him from his parents. An emotionally drained Swarn returned home past 11.00 p. m. and he informed Radha about Abhay. Radha had a nervous breakdown and she fell to the floor. Swarn took care of her for the rest of the night. That entire night they were restless and very worried about the well-being of the child. The next morning, both of them went to Abhay's house and informed his parents about his disappearance. Om Singh was shocked, but he reacted sensibly. However, Sheela Devi, who cared the least for Abhay, shouted the loudest and accused the couple of abducting her son. She forced Om Singh to register an FIR (First Information Report) against Swarn and Radha, and they were booked by the police under the grave charges of child trafficking. They were beaten up badly at the police station to extract their confession but were later let off for the lack of evidence. Their own guilt, and stigma of being declared child traffickers by society, forced Radha and Swarn to leave Nangal Raya and nobody heard anything about them after that. They were rumoured to have committed suicide in shame. No one knew the truth, except God, and Sunita who was Radha's childhood friend. It was almost 5:00 p. m. that evening when Khaani's telephone rang, disrupting the flow of his narration, and she went out to take that call. Thereafter, he saw her rushing to her room. She returned after about half an hour and looked visibly quite disturbed. She tried to smile, not her natural smile, and she said, "Sorry,

I had to take that call. My friend called me after a long time. Please resume, please."

"Okay, one more coffee, and I will resume." When she went to fetch him the coffee, Abhay thought for a moment, and he felt that Khaani was not normal. It was for the second time that day when she deliberately tried to hide things from him. His instincts were calling him once again. She returned with a cup of coffee and, as if gauging his thoughts about the lack of her composure, asked unexpectedly, "What are you thinking?" He looked into her eyes, did not answer her question, smiled, and resumed telling the tale of his life. However, he realised that after the telephone call, Khaani was not as enthusiastic to hear him as she was when he commenced telling his story. Abhay's instinct was right, and her thoughts were straying elsewhere. But where to?!

Niti Village

The train arrived at 7.00 a.m. the next morning at Haridwar Railway Station. Two Toyota SW4 had come to receive Thakur Saheb. Young Abhay had no idea of what was happening. He was asked to sit in one of the SUVs and they drove off to Niti Village. After about five hours of drive on the undulating and wandering mountain road along River Alaknanda, they turned towards Niti Valley. In the Indian Subcontinent, Niti Valley is a remote valley located in the northernmost region of Uttarakhand at a height of 3,600 m (11,811 ft). It is close to the Chinese border and Niti is the last village in the valley before the border with South Tibet. Niti Pass was an ancient trade route between Tibet and India, and it was closed after the 1962 Sino-India War. Since then, the border has remained sealed. Due to adverse weather conditions in the winters, the villages in the valley were only hospitable for about six to eight months. Villagers had to migrate to lower regions during the winters. Abhay was already feeling cold when they reached Niti. As the vehicles entered a big compound and reached a large porch of the Haveli (A haveli is a traditional townhouse, mansion, or manor house in the Indian subcontinent, usually one with historical and architectural significance, and located in a town or city. Haveli was popularised under the Mughal Empire and was devoid of any architectural affiliations.), Abhay was intimidated by the aura and luxury of Thakur Saheb's mansion. That was a multistorey haveli, organised around two large courtyards. The opulent outer courtyard was strictly reserved for meetings and trade while the inner courtyard was home to the family. Abhay was given to the care of Shri Dalpat Singh who was the Maali (Gardener) of the house. Though he missed Radha Kaki, Abhay lived happily with Dalpat Singh and helped him in farming.

Thakur Bodh Pratap Singh Ji Chandel

Thakur Bodh Pratap Singh Ji Chandel was addressed as Thakur Baba in the village. He had lost Thakuraien Sahiba recently and their daughters Nalini and Naveli were two and one year old respectively. Considering the severity of winters in Niti and the tender age of the girls, Thakur Baba had decided to shift to the outskirts of Mussoorie where they owned ten acres of ancestral land. One afternoon, there was a reasonably large get-together in the sprawling lawns of the haveli. Everyone was having fun and Nalini and Naveli were playing with their granny. Abhay was watching the party from behind a tree. When the granny was busy feeding Nalini, Naveli walked towards the pond and went dangerously close to it, her foot slipped, and she fell into the pond. Everyone was in high spirits and nobody noticed her except Abhay. Although Abhay was only five-year-old, he was fiercely protective of both Nalini and Naveli. Abhay ran into the party shouting for help, but his voice was drowned in the din of merry-making. Fearing the wrath of Thakur Baba, and failing to comprehend the gravity of the dangerous situation, the support staff turned him away. A helpless Abhay ran to save Naveli and jumped into the slushy waters. The resultant splash attracted the attention of people and some of them ran to save him. As soon as Abhay reached Naveli, she clung to him tightly thus restricting his movements, and they together started drowning. With great difficulty somehow, he managed to separate her from him and safely brought her to the bank. By then, he was drained out, could not climb the bank, and started sinking in the water. Everyone was taking care of Naveli who was almost fainting with fear and no one as such noticed Abhay till she repeatedly pointed in the direction of the pond. That drew the attention of Thakur Baba to Abhay who was drowning. He immediately rushed, jumped into the pond, and he lifted him up. Since then, Abhay became his son and he moved into the inner courtyard of the Haveli and became a part of the family. Abhay continued to remain protective of Nalini and Naveli, they felt safe in his company and he became their Dada (Elder brother) thereafter.

Abhay Became a Parachute Commando

Soon they shifted to their new bungalow on the outskirts of Mussoorie. Abhay went to school there and later he joined Rashtriya Indian Military College (RIMC) in Doon Valley,

Dehradun. Abhay was a very talented boy, he excelled both academically and in sports. He played all games, but he was very good at boxing, horse riding, and swimming. Abhay remained a topper all along. He topped RIMC, bagged a gold medal at the National Defence Academy (NDA), Khadakwasla, Pune, earned the Sword of Honour at the Indian Military Academy (IMA), Dehradun, got Commando Dragger at the Commando Course, completed the Special Forces (SF) training with distinction, joined the elite 10 Parachute Commando SF, and won a Sena Medal in his very first operation in the insurgency ridden Kashmir Valley.

The First Pay

When Abhay got his first pay after three months of his service, his commanding officer (CO) summoned him and said, "So you got your first pay and arrears of pay. Feeling great?"

"Yes Sir", was his crisp answer.

"And how much are your accumulated stipends from NDA and IMA?"

"Rs. 27 lakh and with arrears of pay I have a total of approximately Rs.30 lakh."

"I have granted you 12 days of casual leave and to-and-fro couriers have been booked for you. Go give 50 percent of your first earnings to your mother, touch her feet, and thank her."

Abhay saluted the CO, went to his hut, with tears in his eyes, wrote the cheque for Rs. 30 lakh in favour of Kamala Singh, and placed it at the feet of their unit deity in the unit mandir (Temple). That uncashed cheque is still held safely in the temple's treasure chest as a mark of his respect for his deceased mother Kamala Singh. The next day he took the flight and reached home in the evening. It was a huge and pleasant surprise for everyone at home. Abhay had come on his first leave after his commission into the Indian Army. Thakur Baba was very happy to see Abhay, and Nalini and Naveli were overjoyed. They had a family get-together that night. There Abhay gave Thakur Baba the cheque of Rs.30 lakh his first earning. Thakur Baba was overwhelmed and hugged him for a long time. They both had tears of joy in their eyes and even Nalini and Naveli came into the family huddle. After some time, Thakur Baba returned the cheque to him and said, "I have always been very proud of you, I am honoured to have you as my son, and I love you. I am sure you love me more. And with that divine Raabta (Connection of souls), I assume the right to return the cheque to you, and before you stray on an emotional turf, listen to me carefully. You know that God has been very kind to us and given us everything that we need in life. Having said this, I must reiterate that you have worked very hard to have earned your honour, dignity, and pride in life on your own. You are a child of life's longing for itself. You are different because you are an excellent human being, and goodness has a price tag attached to it. This is the opportunity to pay the price."

Abhay did not understand anything and he protested, "But, Baba?"

"No, ifs, no buts, do what I say, and I expect you to honour my words. I want you to go to Nangal Raya and give Rs. 7 lakh to your father because he loved your mother and you. Give Rs. 10 lakh to your Radha Kaki and Swarn Kaka. Of the remaining money, give what you want to Nalini, Naveli, and yourself."

Before he could say anything, Naveli said, "Not less than 5 lakh each for Nalini Didi (Elder sister) and me, rest you may keep. Give Baba a good gift." Everyone laughed, but Abhay looked a little worried and he asked Baba, "I have come on leave only for a few days, how will I find Radha Kaki now?"

Thakur Baba replied, "I have located them. They are working as the farm labourers in Tatiri Urban Village in District Baghpat, Meerut."

The next day Abhay returned to a lukewarm welcome at his home in Nangal Raya and met his father. Om Singh was very happy to meet Abhay and he apologised for not being able to take care of him in a manner that was expected of him as his father. His stepmother, for whatever reason, remained somewhat aloof, and his step sisters did not know him. Abhay hugged his father briefly, thanked him for loving his Maa, and requested him to accept the cheque of Rs. 7 lakh as her blessing. Thereafter, he immediately drove off to Tatiri to meet Radha Kaki and Swarn Kaka. Initially, they were intimidated by the aura of Abhay when they saw him as a well-groomed, well-dressed, and well-educated young man who drove an SUV and they couldn't recognise him. However, when he touched their feet and introduced himself, all hesitations simply vanished, and they both hugged him and cried for a long time. That was their first meeting with him after he was separated from them at the New Delhi Railway Station. They couldn't believe their eyes and were overjoyed to meet him. Abhay met both of them wholeheartedly and he requested them to come along with him, but they did not want to dislodge themselves from their dwellings once again. He stayed the night with them in their hut and ate the food so lovingly cooked by Radha Kaki on Chulah (Earthen Stove). The next day he thanked them for everything and persuaded them to accept the cheque of Rs.10 lakh as a token of his love for them. They were overwhelmed by his love, and they showered their blessings upon him with tears of gratitude in their eyes.

And She Shot Him

Khaani pretended to hear him intently and said, "You are a self-made man, I am impressed."

He replied, "I am a God-made man and that's probably the reason you are impressed. Now, let's freshen up, it's already 7:00 p. m., Baba will wait for us to join him for dinner sharp at 8." Even at the dinner table that night, she did not appear normal. Abhay sensed some trouble, and he alerted Sukhbir Singh. After dinner, she came back to his room for giving him the medicines. She stayed on much longer than she normally did and they chatted. It was getting late and she said, "It is already 11.00 p. m., let's sleep we have to go for the morning walk tomorrow."

Abhay saw a shade of sadness in her eyes and as she turned to leave, he went to the washroom. When he returned, he was surprised to see her still standing at the door and pointing Baba's pistol at him. She looked sad, she looked different, and she said, "I am sorry, I don't want to, I can't, but I have to do this" Abhay found her behaviour rather strange; and before he could think any further, she fired at him.

THE REVENGE
AND REPERCUSSIONS

There is no revenge so complete as forgiveness.

– Josh Billings

Rush Abhay to Hospital

Immediately after shooting Abhay, Khaani was gripped in guilt and remorse. She rushed towards him to help him but when she saw a lot of blood on his chest, she was scared and stepped back. Her inner realm was not happy. She knew that Abhay was not wrong, he trusted her, and she had betrayed his trust. That was a sin. He was innocent. She had to go into a deliberate denial, defy her tender feelings for him, hold him guilty, and take her revenge. However, immediately after that dastardly act, her feelings rebelled against her for what she had done to him. She found her act repugnant. There were more questions than answers. But why was she crying? Those were certainly not the tears of joy for accomplishing an impossible mission. Those could be for the release of her pent-up emotions after the successful completion of the assigned task. But it was not so because Khaani knew that she was crying for killing Abhay. Why for Abhay? He was their enemy. Had she fallen in love with the enemy? What were those feelings after he had accidentally touched her hand at the Maggie-Point? Lost in those mixed feelings, she listlessly walked into Thakur Baba's room. The sound of the fire had woken him up and he was in the process of rushing out to check when Khaani entered his room. She was crying, she put the loaded weapon down on his study table, she had no energy to stand and she slumped to the floor. By that time, Nalini and Naveli had also come to his room. Before anyone could ask her anything, she said, "I am sorry, I had to kill Abhay Pratap Singh." All of them were shell-shocked, there was a disquieting silence for a moment before they shouted in unison, "Why? Who are you?" and rushed towards Abhay's room. None of them heard when Khaani pleaded, "Please rush him to the hospital and call the police."

Hala Khan was Arrested

When they entered Abhay's room, they saw him sitting on the chair, he was smiling and there was a lot of blood on his T-shirt. On seeing so much blood on Abhay, Naveli fainted. At that precise moment, Sukhbir entered the room, held her, and said, "Gaddi Laga Di Hai Saheb Ji." (Vehicle is ready, let's go.) To everyone's surprise, a profusely bleeding Abhay walked up to Thakur Baba when he heard him call the police, and he feebly said "No. please don't." But no one heard his voice in those frenetic moments. Nalini and Naveli accompanied Abhay to the hospital, Thakur Baba had to stay at home and wait for the police to arrive. Finally, after an hour or so, the police arrived, ceased Thakur Baba's licensed pistol from which Abhay was shot, and sealed Abhay's room for further forensic examination of the scene of the crime.

They took Hala Khan into custody and escorted her to the police station. When she reached the police station, she was welcomed with a barrage of expletives for hurting a well-known and respected Army officer. She asked for water which was denied to her, she was made to sit on the dusty floor and handcuffed. She stopped crying because she was shocked at the all-male hostility toward her in the police station. She was shivering in the cold when two Mahila (Female) police constables arrived and she felt a bit reassured by the mere presence of the women around her. But that assurance was short-lived because as soon as those ladies arrived, they started abusing her and slapping her beautiful face. She did not know what hit her and why, but surprisingly she felt stronger for perhaps physical torture was the perfect antidote to her mental turmoil. Strange are the ways of God in which lesser external pain kills the greater inner pain.

Candid Confession

Thereafter, perhaps as a supposed consolation and a short respite from the beating, a police inspector pulled up a chair closer to her, signalled the policewomen to stop hitting her, held her from her hair, and pulled her bleeding face up to face him. He asked, "Did you …", and before he could complete his question, she replied, "Yes, I have killed Major Abhay Pratap Singh."

Surprised by her candid confession, the inspector asked, "Why did you do that?"

With a lot of remorse for what she had done and tears in her eyes, she replied, "I did not want to kill him, but I had to.", and she burst out crying.

There was no sympathy for her and the inspector asked her firmly, "Why?"

Hala thereafter maintained a stoic silence and refused to utter a word beyond her confession. Then began the ordeal that was aimed at breaking her silence and resistance. An ordeal, that was going to define unlimited systemic depravity to break her in, but that will never be sufficient to subdue an equally strong will of a fragile-looking strong girl to stick to her stance. The thrashing that began that night was going to be normalised for a long time to come for her. That night she was neither given food nor water and in the wee hours of the morning, an almost unconscious Hala was dragged and pushed into a dingy and dusty cell ridden with insects, lizards, and rodents. She licked her lips wet and pleaded for a drop of water and all she received was a kick in her stomach.

Abhay and Hala were Telling Lies

The next day, police went to record the statement of Major Abhay Pratap Singh at the Military Hospital (MH), Dehradun. Abhay was okay and he was in a good shape. The bullet fired at him miraculously tore only a blood vessel near his right shoulder, which caused excessive bleeding, and the tear was since repaired by an appropriate minor surgical procedure. The inspector saluted him and said, "Janab (A salutation), I am inspector Kuldeep Singh and I have come to record your statement regarding the attempt to murder you the last night."

Abhay was measured in his words when he said, "No, no, it was not an attempt to murder me. The pistol went off accidentally when Hala Khan was taking it from my room to return the same to Thakur Baba. She could never think of killing me, she was a dedicated nurse who cared for me."

"We are looking at a terror angle in the deliberate and well-planned attempt to kill you, Sir."

"I don't think it was a terror plot. Just think of it Inspector Saheb, she had so many opportunities to attack me when I was alone, seriously unwell and she did not.

"But Sir, she has confessed to attacking you last night."

"She is telling a lie. If she wanted to eliminate me, she would have had a strong motive for that."

Motive Remained Elusive

"We'll find that out Sir, thank you.", the inspector said and he left. Kuldeep was an experienced cop and he knew that both Abhay Pratap and Hala Khan were telling lies. He tried hard to understand that puzzle, but he failed to crack that mystery. In his considered assessment, Hala was acting under extreme pressure from her handler. She was perhaps being blackmailed for something precious to her. He could be thinking on the right lines, but the facts on the ground and circumstances were not corroborating to present a coherent picture of the motive of the crime. The results of the forensic examinations confirmed that Hala Khan had indeed fired the weapon to kill Abhay, but the motive remained elusive. The seven days of her sustained interrogation and the accompanying severe torture could not extract the motive of the crime from her. In the meantime, the high-profile case was taken over by the National Investigation Agency (NIA) for a further specialised investigation to explore the terror angle of the attack on Abhay. The NIA Team reached Dehradun to take over the case and custody of Hala Khan. Hala had serious injuries, she had bruises, deep cuts, and a fracture of her left foot. She was running a high fever and she was not in a medically fit state to travel to New Delhi. Accordingly, she had to be admitted to the Government Hospital in Dehradun for medical care.

What Happened That Night

After spending 48 hours at the Military Hospital, Dehradun, Abhay was considered fit for discharge. He still had seven days to go before his sick leave was over. As he came to his room, the memories of the time he spent with Khaani there flooded his mind and a mild smile broke out on his face. He distinctly remembered that the problem began immediately after that 5:00 p. m. phone call. She heard his story with so much interest till then and the way she responded to him made her look even more beautiful. After that phone call when she returned, she heard him alright, but she was not attentive and mostly remained lost in her thoughts. He recollected that she never stayed in his room past 10:00 p. m. post-dinner, on that night, however, she stayed on till 11:00 p. m. After that, he remembered she told him, "It is already 11:00 p. m., let's sleep we have to go for the morning walk tomorrow," or words to that effect. As she wished him goodnight and turned to go to her room, he went to the washroom to freshen up. When he came out after about five minutes, he saw Khaani standing with her back to the closed door of his room and pointing Baba's pistol at him. Abhay's soldierly instincts had prepared him for the danger, but that sudden turn of events surprised him. He tried to smile and said, "Don't play with the weapon, it is loaded, and where did you get it from?"

Abhay saw her trembling, her hands were shaking, tears were flowing from her eyes and she said, "I am sorry, I don't want to, I can't, but I have to do this."

Abhay's mind was working at top speed, he needed to gain time, and snatch the weapon. He asked, "Who called you on phone this evening?"

Khaani was sobbing, not even looking at him, and as if not even listening to him, she fired. Immediately after she shot him, she rushed to help him. However, on seeing the gush of blood flowing on his chest, she got scared, stepped back, and went out of the room. Abhay came back to the moment, tried to take his mind away from her, changed into the night dress, and tried to sleep, but he could not. The thoughts were cluttering his mind. He had a lot of questions to ask himself. Questions like, "Who is Hala Khan? Why did she want to kill him? How did the security system fail? Why was she crying? Why were her hands trembling? Why didn't she kill him? Why did she rush towards him after she fired? Did she love him? "Why did he want to save her and for what? What is that Raabta (Connection of souls)? And most importantly, was he in love with her? With those questions and many thoughts, he went off to sleep.

Time, Memories, and Hope Travel Together

When his sick leave ended, he reported to the Army Hospital, Srinagar on the due date. He was temporarily placed in a lower medical category and offered a soft posting to a non-operational area. Abhay was a crack commando; he could not imagine himself being away from the scene of action even for a moment and as such he declined the offer of a soft posting.

Till such time his medical category was upgraded, he served at the operational headquarters of his unit at Pattan. Abhay was a bright and brave officer whose professional acumen was extraordinary. Time flew and in the next five years or so, he rose in ranks, was promoted to the coveted rank of the commanding officer, and he assumed the command of elite 10 Para Cdo (SF) in Kashmir valley. Khaani never deserted his thoughts and he could not imagine spending his life with anyone else except her. He had lost contact with her, but not the connection, and he hoped to meet her soon. On the family front, Nalini and Naveli did well in their respective professions and they made Thakur Baba and him very proud. They were married and happily settled in life. Sukhbir Singh was promoted too, to become Subedar Major of the unit under Abhay's competent command.

TRIAL AND TRIBULATIONS

*Sometimes the questions are
complicated and the answers are simple.*

She is Not Talking

It took some 12 days for Hala to recover in the hospital. Thereafter, NIA brought her to New Delhi and her case was assigned to Assistant Commissioner of Police (ACP) Shri Sangram Singh who was known to be a brash and unorthodox officer in his methods of investigations. That man was very wily, and with his trademark fragile ego, he could go to any extreme to crack the case. Surprisingly, he was awkwardly soft in his approach in the case of Hala. He was rumoured to be infatuated with her. On the contrary, his assistant, Senior Inspector Supriya Subramanian was a quite sober, sensible, and intelligent officer. Having been accustomed to the torture she faced at the hands of Dehradun Police, Hala was mentally prepared to face the investigations and an increasing degree of difficulties. Sangram was quite surprised at a fragile-looking Hala's tenacity to withstand so much beating and humiliation, and yet fiercely stick to her stance against all odds. He discussed that with Supriya and she simply advised, "Sir, let's stick to the fundamentals and approach the case normally. Who knows, she may be just a pawn in the hands of the terrorists? Maybe, she is innocent. Maybe, she is not."

"But why is she not talking?", he quipped.

"She will, let's begin."

The Interrogation Began

They began and worked on the known themes of investigations for such cases hoping to break the will of Hala Khan and crack the case. She had a rather uneventful day and her experience told her that it was a premonition of the future storm that would hit her hard. Finally, at 8.00 p.m., she was summoned to the NIA's investigation chamber. There was a large table in the centre of the room, a chair, and one bench. There was also an earthen waterpot on a stand in the corner of the room with a steel glass chained to the stand. There was no ventilation in that room, and the CCTV cameras were in place to record the proceedings. Hala waited, and she waited for more than two hours. That waiting was terrible and she braced up for the anticipated brutality on the other side of the wait. And in the adjoining room, Sangram and Supriya were reading every expression on her face. At approximately 11.00 p.m., one young woman, dressed in the western formals, came in and placed a laptop in front of Hala, and asked, "Do you play computer games?"

A bit intrigued, Hala replied, "No."

"Lies don't work here. Your mobile phone had multiple access to various gaming sites and we know all about that."

Hala kept mum, but the lady spoke, "Have fun while it lasts and play on this laptop. There is a questionnaire, keep answering the same, and don't stop till the time you are told to stop."

Hala began answering those unending questions some of which would repeat randomly. The computer programme did not permit her to go back and amend the answers that she had already given earlier. That process went on continuously till 3.00 a. m. in the morning, with one washroom and one water break each. Every time she fell asleep, she was rudely shaken by the lady constables on duty. Fortunately, she was not slapped, not even once since she was taken into NIA's custody. At around 3.00 a.m., she was told to stop and taken to her solitary cell. Her cell was very small and it had nothing in it, not even water. That did not bother her. As soon as she was pushed into the cell, she fell on the dusty floor, and she slept like a log. Supriya came to her cell, looked at Hala, and she smiled, a mysterious smile for whatever reasons.

She was Consistent

Hala's answers were critically examined at the Information Technology (IT) Cell of NIA and surprisingly, there were no inconsistencies in them. There was a definite pattern that indicated that probably Hala could be telling the truth and she was mentally alert. The next morning, she was rudely woken up, but surprisingly given access to a cleaner washroom. She had tea and toast before she was summoned to the Investigation room at sharp 8.00 a. m. Although her clothes were shabby, she looked quite refreshed. Her interrogation commenced immediately thereafter and the first question came from Sangram, and he asked, "Where is your home?"

Her answer was crisp and she said, "Srinagar."

"Give correct and full address."

"C/O Shri Mir Haadi, 7/86, Residency Road, Lal Chowk, Srinagar. Hania Saeed and Sana Khan had rented a room in that house and I shared that with them."

"But we checked that house, it is deserted. Where have Shri Mir Haadi and your friends gone?"

"I have no idea, Sir, and Hania and Sana are not my friends."

"Your Aadhaar Card gives your permanent address at Rahimabad and that is a fake address. Who are you?"

"I am Hala Khan, daughter of Shri Javed Khan."

"Why did you kill Abhay?"

"I killed him because he was killing innocent Muslims."

"But you loved him."

Hala was surprised by that statement for two reasons. One, she was not sure whether she loved Abhay, and two, she had never shared her feelings for him with anyone. Just then her thought went to the answers she had given in the NIA questionnaire and she understood the NIA statement. She was in those thoughts when Supriya again asked, "Are you in love with Major Abhay Pratap Singh?"

She did not know why, but replied, "Yes, I love him and will continue to love him because he was Allah's blessing to me."

"Why did you kill Allah's blessing?"

"I did so because Allah is bigger than his blessings and he knows the best."

Incomplete Story

The questioning continued for about a week and the summary of what Hala told them was, "She was tasked to kill Major Abhay Pratap Singh by Mullah Akhbar alias Feroze Khan who met her in Dargah Sharif. He told her that Abhay was a Kaafir and he was killing innocent Muslims. The plan was to poison Major Abhay while he was being treated at the Army Hospital, Srinagar. Hania and Sana kept the poison vials that were given to her by her handler, and they were the backup for her for the operation code-named, "Operation Qaatil". Mullah Akhbar alias Feroze Khan was her handler, maybe lover, and he was based in Neelum Valley of Pakistan Occupied Kashmir (POK). When she saw Abhay for the first time, she hated him, however, for some unknown reasons, later she fell in love with him. She had many opportunities to poison him, but she just did not do that. On that fateful night also, she did not want to fire at him, but somehow the weapon went off and Abhay was killed." They assessed that Hala Khan, under duress, was telling lies and she had probably concocted stories to conceal the truth. But the consistency of her thoughts was indeed amazing. Most disturbing, however, was that she believed she loved Abhay despite everything for some divine connection of the past, and her belief appeared to be genuine. She fondly remembered Thakur Baba, Nalini, and Naveli, and the time she spent with them and Abhay at the Army Hospital, Srinagar, and later at their home near Mussoorie. She thought she had killed Abhay and she was most miserable and remorseful for that."

With Hala's rigid stance and the consistency of her statement, the case had hit a dead end. All the techniques of interrogation had failed to get Hala to tell the truth. No one knew the truth, but NIA wanted her to tell their truth. She remained stuck to a story that was deemed false by NIA, and the investigations were going nowhere. They approached the Delhi High Court for Polygraph and Hala came out clean there also. There were sufficient indicators of Hala's involvement in attacking Abhay as part of a major terror plot, but those were not supported by the evidence. Abhay was the sole eyewitness and he had stated that he was injured in an accidental fire.

Bright Officer went Berserk

The failure to bring the case to a logical conclusion hurt ACP Sangram Singh's ego rather hard, and under tremendous pressure from the top to solve the case in a given timeframe, he crossed all the limits of human abjection and unleashed the horror of brutality on a hapless Hala Khan. She was beaten day in and day out. Her whole body was broken and bruised, but her spirit stood strong. That angered him even more. Everyone at the NIA cell wondered why Hala was being continuously exposed to the gross human depravity when she had already confessed to her crime. Inhumanity, in any case, was unjustifiable. Most of the staff were worried about her safety while in NIA's custody and they had sympathy for her. Intending to protect her from the wrath of the ACP, they locked her cell from the outside at night because Sangram Singh usually came past midnight to torture Hala. That night also an inebriated Sangram barged in past midnight, and on seeing her cell locked, he lost his cool, crossed all limits of insanity, and picked up a baton to attack Hala. He ordered the staff on duty to open the lock of Hala's cell. When the staff cited the orders of the DCP Niveditha Aiyar to the contrary and refused to follow his orders, he broke open the lock and immediately started hitting a half-dead Hala mercilessly. By then Hala had become so numb by the daily bouts of severe battering that leave aside shrieks, that she did not even utter a sigh of pain and simply endured that heartless onslaught of brutality on her battered body with rare courage and dignity. Perhaps, the physical pain beyond a point ceases to have an effect. Hala appeared to have gone beyond the threshold of that pain point where inhumanity was not sufficient to force her to say what he wanted to hear, and that frustrated Sangram further. He dropped the blood-stained baton and dragged an almost dead Hala by her hair towards him and started touching her inappropriately with a view to outrage her modesty. Hala did not react; she was unconscious and had no idea of what he was doing to her body. By that time, Supriya had informed Ms. Niveditha Aiyar, Deputy Commissioner of police about the incident. Having done that, she rushed to save Hala, and pushed Sangram away from her, thereby inviting his wrath on herself. He left Hala for a moment and attacked Supriya, but she overpowered him with the help of the staff on duty. Just then, Niveditha walked in and ordered the arrest of ACP Sangram Singh. That incident shocked the entire staff on duty that day. Nobody could imagine that one of their finest officers was so defeated by a tough stance of a fragile and helpless young girl that not only did he beat her up mercilessly but even had no hesitation in attempting to rape her in full public view that night. Infinity is the limit of depravity and stupidity.

Terror Angle

Hala had to be evacuated in a critical condition to All India Institute of Medical Sciences (AIIMS), New Delhi and she was directly taken into an ICU. She had suffered multiple fractures, deep cuts, and internal bleeding. Fortunately, with multiple corrective surgeries and intensive medical care she survived. But she remained hospitalised for over three months. A departmental inquiry constituted to investigate the incident, found ACP Sangram Singh guilty of gross misconduct, and recommended termination of his service with immediate effect, and initiation of criminal proceedings against him. That was indeed a sad day because after being pronounced guilty by the departmental inquiry when he was leaving for home, he was shot dead by two unidentified youths right in front of NIA Headquarters. That further complicated the proceedings of Hala's case because the killing of ACP Sangram Singh almost confirmed the terror angle to her case. Concurrently, Hala's lawyers successfully appealed and got the order to transfer Hala to Tihar Jail after her recovery and discharge from AIIMS. NIA did not oppose and recommended her trial from Tihar Jail itself. With the available evidence, she was charged under the relevant sections of IPC (Indian Penal Code) for culpable homicide with the intent to kill.

Dandelions

Struggles are required in order to survive in life because in order to stand up, you got to know what falling down is like.

Her Feelings Found Her Again

With very competent, comprehensive, and intensive care at the hospital, Hala was able to move on her own after about two months. She had recovered well, and she was shifted out of ICU to the Prisoners' ward. Although Hala was progressing well, she still needed a lot of care and proper rehabilitation for a complete recovery before she could be considered to be fit for discharge. Ms. Jasmina Kire was the sister in charge of the ward and she was a very compassionate young lady. She was from Marima, a village near Kohima in Nagaland. Somehow, she liked Hala from the day they met, they gelled really well with each other, and over time they became friends. Hala was in such a delicate state of mind where physical pain had no meaning for her, but affection and love would make her cry. Jasmina could understand her condition and she took care to ensure that her emotional vulnerability did not hamper the process of her healing. Another thing that happened to Hala was that for the first time after her arrest, she had time to think and connect to her feelings once again. And when she connected to herself, she realised that most of the time she did not think about her mother, father or brother, or even her future because the thoughts of Major Abhay Pratap Singh dominated her mind space. She did feel guilty about killing him, but never for loving him. She could not fathom what bound her to him. Sometimes she felt, Abhay would hate her for betraying his trust. Then, the very next moment, she would remember many of his tender gestures which bore the authenticity of his love for her. She believed she would get a death sentence for her heinous crime, but somewhere in her heart, she wanted to live only with and for him. That was a strange state of her mind that kept her caged in her thoughts about him and she felt happy to be in them despite facing the most uncertain future.

Happiness Outweighs Pain

One evening when Hala was sitting in the corridor outside her ward and delving into her inner thoughts, Jasmina just walked in and surprised her. Hala looked at her, smiled, and asked, "What are you doing here, your shift was over in the morning?"

Jasmina had a counter-question, "Why can't I spend some more time with you? You have any objection?"

"Never, you are like a fresh lease of life for me. I think we share some divine bond between us."

"I have shared all that I had in my life with you, my family, my love affairs, my successes, and my failures. But what about you?"

Hala said, "I have told you about my parents, my brother, and all other things that I did not tell Dehradun police and NIA even after some sound thrashing that I received from them."

"What about your love?"

"Let my troubles be over, I will hide nothing from you even if you depose against me later in a court of law."

"I feel terrible about your sufferings. You are just 20 years old and life has really ill-treated you beyond words."

"There are two things to it. First, life has its own unique ways for each one of us and it takes us on the tracks that would help us later. I have no complaints about life. Look the life loved me for 19 years, and she reserves the right to correct me when I make mistakes. And the second, life in all fairness balances pains with happiness, and vice versa. Let me tell you, happiness always weighs heavier than pain because the nature of nature is happiness."

"Where did you get the strength to bear unlimited pain that has been inflicted upon you by the system?"

"Pain never goes in vain and beyond a threshold, pain becomes pleasurable."

"How? Explain."

Before Hala could say further, Amar Bhaiya (Brother), ward boy, brought steaming cups of tea and biscuits for them. They thanked him, Hala smiled and said, "See, happiness is here and now."

They laughed, but Jasmina persisted with her question.

Pain Never Goes in Vain

Hala said philosophically, "The moment you come to terms with pain, it becomes agreeable like pessimism and it culminates in universal acceptance. Pain is always cathartic. It binds you with the rest of mankind. Unless one feels the pangs of pain, one cannot love wholeheartedly, because pain cleanses the doors of perceptions and gives perspicuous clarity to the sufferer; Pain never goes in vain because once it is internalised, it ennobles, enlightens, and finally, emancipates you from all quotidian and everyday concerns. Life's all joys are tainted with pain. I am a graduate of English literature and I must quote Poet P B Shelley who famously said, 'Our laughter with some pain is fraught/Our sweetest songs are those that tell of the saddest thought.' Happiness is but an occasional episode in the painful drama of life. Only by accepting the melancholy of life can we enjoy the mirth and merriment of living." Jasmina was amazed at the depth of her knowledge, but she did not try to interrupt her flow. She just smiled, Hala smiled too, and continued, "American sage Ralph Waldo Emerson says, 'A man who took great pride in his lawn, found himself with a large crop of dandelions. He tried every method he knew to destroy them. Still, they plagued him. Finally, he wrote to the department of agriculture. He enumerated all the things that he had tried and closed his letter with the question, 'What shall I do now?' In due course, the reply came, 'We suggest you learn to love them."

"For your age, Hala your knowledge is amazing."

"I never wanted to know this, but life had to teach me the harsher way in the past one year of my life. Unfortunately, the wisdom was forced on me. And you know what, wisdom and pain are the best friends"

"You see there is a beautiful song Dandelions, sung by Ruth B. We sang that song in chorus in our Marima Church on the last Christmas Eve."

"Why not sing a few lines?"

Dandelions Song

"It's a long song, but I will try to hum a few lines to cheer you up." Jasmina recollected the song for a while and thereafter started singing softly.

"Maybe it's the way you say my name,

Maybe it's the way you play your game,

But it's so good, I've never known anybody like you,

But it's so good, I've never dreamed of nobody like you.

And I've heard of a love that comes once in lifetime,

And I'm pretty sure that you are the love of mine.

'Cause I'm in a field of dandelions,

Wishing on everyone that you'll be mine, mine,

And I see forever in your eyes,

I feel okay when I see you smile, smile,

Wishing on dandelions all of the time,

Praying to God that one day you'll be mine,

Wishing on dandelions all the time, all the time,

I think that you are the one for me,

'Cause, it gets so hard to breathe,

When you're looking at me, I've never felt so alive and free,

When you're looking at me, I've never felt so happy,

And I've heard of a love that comes once in a lifetime,

And I'm pretty sure that you are that love of mine ...

Jasmina stopped singing, looked at Hala who was thoroughly enjoying the song, and said, "It's a long song, I remembered only half of it."

"But that was sufficient for me to realise that I would go with the sound advice of the American department of agriculture, and accept the Dandelions of my life. I know my pains will go, and I know my love too will emerge from the Dandelions of my happiness."

SOME STRANGERS ARE NOT STRANGERS

Obviously, you can't replicate an experience like meeting someone unexpectedly while travelling and developing a once-in-a-life connection bolstered by whimsy, unfamiliarity, and serendipity.

Sleeping With the Enemy

Hala was impressed by both the song and the gesture of Jasmina in making her feel so good and she said, "There was no music, that's good because your melodious voice stood out when you sang Dandelions. I loved it, and it was like wish fulfilment for a dying girl."

Jasmina just hugged her, and suddenly realised what Hala had just said, and she still felt she was joking. And jokingly she asked, "What else is the wish of the dying girl?"

"I want to sleep with the enemy before I die. But that's not possible."

Jasmina realised that Hala was serious and she asked, "Why should you die?"

"I am accused of killing an Army officer as a part of a larger terror plan, of which I have no clue, and the Indian state won't settle for anything lesser than a death penalty for me for my crime."

"Jasmina felt very sad, but she still asked, "And who is your enemy? Why do you want to sleep with your enemy?

"Major Abhay Pratap is the enemy I wanted to sleep with. Alas, that's not going to be possible."

"But why?"

"I love him, and I have killed him. I killed him only to realise that in killing one enemy, the whole world has become my enemy, and that whole includes me and not him."

"You loved Abhay?"

"Yes, and I have even told this to NIA. They don't believe. I am sure you do."

"Naturally, why would they? You don't kill those you love."

"Strange are the ways of Abhay's God, your Jesus Christ, and my Allah. You see Jasmina, you can run, but you can't hide. I wish, Abhay's God was my God."

"But why?"

"His God allows rebirth and that way my death could bridge the gap between our worlds in our next birth."

Just then, the sister on duty came and informed Jasmina that the doctors were coming for the rounds and Hala should return to the ward. They waved at each other and parted for the day. Later that night, Hala was thinking of Abhay for a long time. She remembered those small moments that brought her closer to him. Yes, she was in love with him, but why?

Does Allah want her to fall in love with him? Does Abhay love her? What is the future of her feelings for him especially when the media trials have all pronounced her to be a dreaded LeT terrorist? Why was she thinking about him? Is he alive? Those were some of the disturbing questions that haunted Hala that night. But they failed to subdue her feelings for him.

Jasmina Kire

Suddenly, her thoughts switched to Jasmina. She never met her before. What compelled her to open up to her? Do they share some unbroken bond? She was sure that they both had an emotionally cheering relationship that tapped into their primal feelings about money, power, pleasure, shame, intimacy, everything; and love as a redemptive power. They were total strangers with a different family, geographic, and bringing-up backgrounds, till they met at AIIMS. That was a case of a strange relationship between Jasmina who was a government employee and Hala, a deemed terrorist, who was an enemy of the state. She had no answer, so she conveniently passed that on Allah's wish once again. But she couldn't stop the flow of her thoughts on the emotional intimacy between them. She thought, "She, for sure, had experienced a special connection with Jasmina. The kind of connection, which was hard to describe, but impossible to overcome. Different sciences tried to explain that phenomenon, emphasising different channels of such bonding. Psychologists said that came from deep understanding, others considered the frequency of their thinking as the main reason, and some of them believed it was the magical power of love. All of them were partly right. She saw how lyrical and profound her most momentary connection broadened her understanding and deepened her perception of Jasmina who was a stranger till recently. She saw the invisible mechanics and meaning of their interactions. That was a new way to be in love with the world. She discovered the unexpected pleasures and exciting possibilities of talking to people she didn't know. Her connection with Jasmina revealed how simple, surprising encounters with strangers pushed her towards greater openness and tolerance, and how those fleeting but powerful emotional connections could change her, and the world that she shared."

Unexpected Connections

The flow of her thoughts was disturbed when the nurse came and gave her an injection. She tried to sleep, but her interesting encounters with Jasmina again took her to the arena where the strangers meet and share happiness. She resumed thinking, "We live in an increasingly insular world. Our heads are down, we're in a hurry, our minds elsewhere. She certainly discovered the surprising pleasures and transformative possibilities in her conversations with her. She found unexpected happiness, genuine emotional connections, and even liberating moments with her. She discovered how those brief interactions made her feel happy, and even understood, and changed how she related to people who are different from her. For her, those fleeting interactions were important interruptions in the disrupted routine of her life, pulling her into experiences of shared humanity and cementing her relationships with the places she lived and worked and played. Those astute cultural analyses, emotional exploration, and powerful vignettes from her own experiences of talking to that stranger Naga girl revealed how those deceptively simple moments could change the way she would interact with the world thereafter." Engrossed in those deep thoughts, she drifted into a deep sleep.

Bonds Transcend Births

On another horizon, Awargi was scanning through Hala's thoughts and sharing them with Ehad who was sitting with her. Ehad began their conversation when she said, "Nusrat is right in her assessment of her Raabta with a stranger but both of them carried that bond from their past light cone and they were blissfully unaware. In fact, they would never know."

"What do you mean by that?", asked Awargi.

"Do you know who is Nusrat?"

"No."

"She was Jasmina's mother in the past light cone?"

"What are you saying?"

"Yes, Jasmina was Maani in her past life and she was Nusrat's daughter who was very deeply attached to her mother. Saral died and Maani was left all alone. And look at the coincidence, they parted in a hospital in Delhi, and then met as strangers in their third birth in a hospital only and that too in the same city. That's the reason that Nusrat and Jasmina bonded so well."

"Strange are the ways of God Almighty, and encounters of the souls bring in familiar bonds, they are beautiful, and yet unknown."

"True, memories cannot transgress light cones and births; bonds do, and they are felt as well. However, sane people don't look for a reason when no reason is the reason for their bonding."

Discharged and Sent to Tihar Jail

Hala was recovering well, and the date of her discharge was approaching fast. One day, Jasmina bought a beautiful salwar-suit for her from the Sarojini Nagar Market and gave it to her. Hala felt touched by the gesture because she did not have any dress of her own except the one that the hospital gave her, and that would be taken away on her discharge. She was sad also because that was a parting gift. She was discharged on the due date, and police took her into their custody for escorting her to Tihar Jail. Jasmina hugged her for a long time before a policewoman separated them. Hala was looking beautiful and she was wearing the same dress that Jasmina gave her when she was handcuffed and shoved into the waiting police van. Jasmina had tears in her eyes and she noticed those policewomen were unreasonably harsh to Hala. But Hala did not fail to smile and wave at her before she was taken away. Jasmina wanted to run to her and hug her once again, but she held herself back.

THE TIHAR JAIL

The hardest prison to escape is in our own minds.

The Brand Tihar

While the police van trudged through the Delhi traffic, Hala noticed that all the policewomen had a kind of frown on their faces. She thought, "I am the one who has been ill-treated, beaten, and brutalised, and the irony of the fate is that those women in uniform were looking so sad. Life does not spare anyone and maintains equanimity of pain for everyone, only the context and circumstances vary. But why are they so angry?" She shook those thoughts out and braced up for the next round of ordeal that life had in store for her at the Tihar Jail. She had read a lot about the improvements at the Tihar Jail and that was very encouraging. She had read that the Tihar prison, also called Tihar Jail was located in Tihar Village, approximately 3 km from Janakpuri, to the West of New Delhi. The prison was styled as a correctional institution. Its main objective was to convert its inmates into ordinary members of society by providing them with useful skills, education, and respect for the law. It aimed to improve their self-esteem and strengthen their desire to improve. To engage, rehabilitate, and reform its inmates, Tihar used music therapy, which involved music training sessions and concerts. The prison had its own radio station, run by inmates. There was also a prison industry within the walls, manned wholly by inmates, which bore the brand Tihar. Finally, after a long and painful drive through the traffic, the police van reached the Tihar complex. Hala was handed over by the police to women jail guards, she crossed through a narrow entrance, and she was immediately taken for a detailed medical cum security check. She was stripped naked for a prolonged and intrusive physical check. That was more of a fondling riot than a proper medical examination. That process lasted almost an hour before she was taken to a small office-type complex for some documentation. Her dress was deposited there and she was given a prison uniform to wear. The uniform was greyish white with deep blue stripes, and that did not fit her properly. She was looking so funny that she smiled looking at herself in that ill-fitting jail dress. Thereafter, she was taken to her cell. That was a small room which she was to share duly cramped up with 8 hardcore criminals. That afternoon itself, she was interviewed by ACP Roshni Sharma, in charge of, the women's prison. She was a fairly decent lady who explained to her the philosophy of Tihar Jail and also told her the dos and don'ts during her stay in the prison.

Reality Strikes Early

However, the reality struck her the same evening when after a roll-call, she went to the kitchen to have her food. That was a shabbily maintained community kitchen run by a prisoners' mafia of sorts. In her turn, when she reached the food counter, she could not help making a face at the lack of general hygiene there. Unfortunately, that was observed by the old lady who was in charge and the mafia don there. She signalled the counter woman not to serve food to her. Hala protested, requested, and literally begged for food. But she was denied food and the jail guards kept mum. No one helped her and she had to go hungry that night. She was denied food for the next two consecutive days as well. Seema Kala, a fellow prisoner secretly shared her food with Hala. On the fourth day, Hala had to apologise and she was served food thereafter. Despite the tall claims of improvement, Tihar Prison was a sad story, especially for women inmates. All women there had sad stories to share, but societal hypocrisy and an indifferent criminal justice system converted them into hardened criminals and heartless humans. Everyone there had forgotten happiness and smile, and they made life miserable for themselves and others in one way or the other.

The Sad State of Affairs

The prisoners were divided into various groups who were fiercely protective of their respective domains and they often indulged in bloody territorial scuffles. In addition to that, the rampant corruption, prison politics, and shipment of drugs, knives, and mobile phones, had taken over the sanity and sensibility of the prison space. Any hints of decency and simplicity instantly attracted the wrath of the system. There were three highly active groups – The kitchen mafia was headed by a harsh and heartless Sunila Devi, besides that, there were two gangs each led by Nayantara and Asma Beg, and there were frequent bloody brawls between them to protect their respective territories. Then there was another group of prisoners called the Dadi gang. That was led by one Jamna

Devi, who was 60-year-old and was serving a life sentence for murdering two men. She was respected by everyone for her strength, sobriety, and magnanimity. That was mostly a dormant group that did not meddle in jail affairs, did not accept any nonsense from anyone, and there was a certain level of maturity in that group. Dadi somehow liked Hala and was quite protective of her. She always encouraged Hala, and told her that Allah loved her, she must trust him, and her troubles would be over soon. The reality of the Tihar Jail was not confined to the community kitchen alone. The shabby community washrooms were hotbeds of drugs, illegal mobile telephony, and lesbian relationships. Even the male jail guards preyed on young women prisoners and sexually exploited them by granting them petty favours. Such sexual liaisons were not always one-sided. Many sexually starved females willingly had sex with young guards in the secluded guard rooms and even quiet corners outdoors. Young and beautiful Hala Khan was an attraction of lust of both men and women alike, she was often touched inappropriately, and her resistance always resulted in severe beatings for her. At times, she was beaten so badly that she had to be admitted to the prison hospital for the treatment of her wounds. Both Nayantara and Asma Beg were hugely powerful ugly fat women, and both of them wooed Hala to be their wife. Hala was not physically strong enough to protect her modesty but she was mentally robust enough to resist such indecent proposals. The redeeming factor was the rivalry between Nayantara and Asma, which often led to serious scuffles between them over her, and saved Hala many times from them. The Dadi Group also saved her many times. However, that was not a solution and she had to be prepared to defend herself against their lecherous designs every day.

Hala Fights Back

Nayantara adopted a softer approach towards Hala, but Asma Beg assumed her right over the affection of Hala because, being a Muslim, she was from her community. Hala was genuinely scared of both of them and she spent a lot of time with Dadi and felt safe in her company. However, one-night Asma Beg, with the help of some corrupt jail guards cornered Hala in a secluded and deserted room. Asma beat her up, broke her resistance, and started raping her ruthlessly. In those painful moments when Hala was about to give up the fight, thoughts of Abhay flashed through her mind. She heard him say, "I love you Khaani. Get up and fight." Surprisingly, that gave her a lot of strength. She pushed Asma away, freed herself, picked up an iron rod lying nearby, and started hitting an inebriated Asma Beg repeatedly. Asma did not know what had hit her and she ran towards the prison courtyard to save herself. But Hala, as if possessed by some spirit, chased her down and kept hitting her. The resultant commotion woke up other inmates, they gathered together and watched a courageous Hala thrashing Asma. Asma was bleeding profusely, begging Hala to spare her life, and when Hala did not relent, she cried for help. Her gang rushed to save her, but they were countered by Nayantara's gang. Hala kept hitting Asma even after she was dead. When that news reached Dadi, she immediately rushed to the courtyard and snatched the rod from Hala. Dadi's friends took Hala away from the scene of the crime, washed her, changed her blood-stained clothes, and asked her to keep quiet. When the jail guards finally arrived, they saw Dadi murdering Asma, and she confessed to killing Asma Beg. Dadi was already serving a life sentence for two murders and hence the third murder did not affect her status as such.

She was arrested yet again, but in doing so she saved Hala. Everyone knew the truth, but of sheer respect for her, and her huge gesture, no one spoke about it. Hala's action elevated her to a status where no one bothered her anymore. She mostly spent time with Dadi's group thereafter.

The Case Stagnates

Deputy Commissioner of Police (DCP) Jehangir Khan, was the overall in charge of the Tihar Jail. He was a good man. He knew the truth about Asma Beg, but he wanted to help Hala because he had understood that the hapless young Kashmiri girl was a victim of the circumstances and system. The system was hostile towards her and LeT was gunning for her. One day he called Hala and advised her to stay sensibly in the Jail and don't add any more charges to the ones already levelled against her. She told him that she was not a habitual criminal and she endeavoured to spend her time in jail responsibly pending her likely death sentence for murdering an Army officer. Jehangir Khan was surprised that she was not even aware that Colonel Abhay Pratap was alive and he was in fine fettle. When he informed her about Abhay, she almost froze, but her heartbeats went into a frenzy, and she bent in gratitude and reverence for Allah. When that information sank in, it was as if she got a fresh lease of life, she shed the burden of her remorse, and felt feather-light. Her strong will to live and love resurfaced. She cried her heart out, and those most certainly were the tears of the bliss of being in Ishq with Allah. She could not imagine any possibility of her union with Abhay, however, a feeble desire to see him, maybe once, gave her a ray of hope and satisfaction. Love healed her injured soul.

Abhay is Alive

The progress of her case was rather tardy and she was languishing in jail for the past four years. All Jehangir Khan could do was expedite the conclusion of the case one way or the other. He moved his contacts and got the case on track. That was quite a typical case where the crime was committed, but the motive was blurred, the evidence inconclusive, and there were no eye witnesses except Colonel Abhay Pratap Singh himself. Long after examining all the witnesses and available evidence, the case could not be concluded without the testimony of Abhay who could not be present in NIA court for numerous operational commitments and the case continued to stagnate. Hala would be taken for every hearing, she would wait for Abhay and when he did not turn up, she would return to jail disappointed. As far as Hala was concerned, knowing that Abhay was alive was her greatest happiness, and for her, seeing Abhay was more important than his testimony which she knew would anyway go against her. That was the scene for every subsequent hearing and the case just got stuck up. Jehangir Khan was not happy, and he was not the man who would give up without trying. So, one day he took the flight to Srinagar and met Abhay. He apprised Abhay about Hala and requested him to come and depose in the court whichever way and allow Hala to move on in her life. Abhay assured him that he would be present for the next hearing of the case.

Love is Crazy

Abhay was very happy to hear about Khaani after five years, but he managed to hold his emotions remarkably well in front of the DCP. He felt that Jehangir Khan was an angel of God

Almighty who had come to pave the path that would take him back to Khaani once again. It was something more than a mere coincidence that he saw his now by far the familiar dream the night before Jehangir Khan was to meet him. There, he once again saw a glimpse of that beautiful girl who was known to him, but he could not recognise her. That face was so familiar, but unknown. Jehangir Khan's visit yet again brought a stream of memories of the beautiful time he spent with Khaani. She was so innocent and she sincerely cared for him. She was loved by Baba, Nalini, and Naveli, but then she shot him. He distinctly remembered that her hands were not steady, they were trembling, and she was crying. He heard her plead repeatedly, "Allah please, I am sorry, I don't want to, I can't, but I have to do this." She definitely did not look at him when she fired the weapon. He looked at her and that was for the first time ever he saw love for him in her beautiful eyes. That was pure love devoid of any traces of indifference. Did she love him? Why did she fire at him? Why was she crying? Why did she go to Baba and surrendered instead of running away? All such questions haunted Abhay when he thought of Khaani, and most of the time she stayed in his thoughts. He felt that she had acted under some serious compulsions, and she was wrong but he still loved her. Baba, Nalini, and Naveli did not agree with him and they would never approve of his love for a traitor who attempted to kill him. She was a Muslim. She was an enemy of their country. Even Sukhbir was against his irrational affection for her. No one wanted him to love an enemy, a liar who betrayed everyone's trust. But Abhay loved her. He wanted to go to the court not only to record his statement but also to get a glimpse of her. Love, for sure, is crazy.

Contradictions

Hala's case was quite different and it was self-contradictory as well. NIA had the clinching evidence that she fired a bullet at Abhay. They, however, could neither establish her intent nor motive to kill him. Yet she was charged under the relevant sections of IPC for culpable homicide with an intent to murder Abhay. Similarly, no conspiracy or terror angle could be proved. Abhay was alive, but she thought she had killed him, and deserved the death penalty for her offence. The contradictions and legality notwithstanding, she mechanically went for all the court hearings for over four years and wondered why she was being spared the death sentence. All that changed when she learnt that Abhay was alive, he was well and she was happy. But she knew that her union with him was most unlikely, especially after what she had done to him and his family. Surprisingly, she still wanted death for her because she thought that was a possible way to be with Abhay in her next birth even though her faith did not have any concept of rebirth or cycle of births. That was a kind of a fog of human understanding through which her love shone. She often said to herself that she was a devout Muslim, but what's that got to do with her love and whatever that happens to her after her death? On the due date, her case had come for a hearing once again. Hala was taken to the NIA Court and as usual, she waited in the police van till she was summoned into the courtroom. She hardly had any expectations from the repeated court hearings, but this time she was oblivious to the surprise that awaited her in the very same courtroom.

THE TESTIMONY

"*One day you will ask me which is more important? My life or yours? I will say mine and you will walk away not knowing that you are my life.*"

– Khalil Gibran

The Happy Feelings

Colonel Abhay Pratap Singh was in time for his testimony in the NIA Court that day He came accompanied by Nalini, Naveli, his protection team, and the memories of his dream of the last night where he again had a glimpse of that beautiful, but an unknown girl. The Public Prosecutor (PP) had already briefed him on the case and his statement to be given in court. NIA Court that day was filled to its capacity, his eyes were eagerly searching for Khaani who was nowhere to be seen, and he was getting anxious. Finally, there was some hustle and bustle in the court as Hala was brought to the court duly handcuffed and escorted by the policewomen. As usual, she looked down, did not look up, and stood quietly in the accused's corner of the court. She looked up only when Abhay was called to the witness box. Suddenly the sparkle in her eyes was restored and her eyes kept following him till he reached the witness box. She continued looking at him even as she said a silent prayer to thank Allah for keeping her Abhay alive. For once, she requested Allah to keep her alive too. She wanted to live for Abhay. As the Public Prosecutor rose to question Abhay, he partly covered him from her view. She looked around and noticed Nalini and Naveli sitting in the spectators' gallery and they seemed to be angry with her. She also saw Jasmina who showed her thumbs-up sign and a smile broke out on her face. Hala had got her smile back after a long time when she came to know about Abhay. She was happy that Abhay was alive. Her happy feelings were hampered by the NIA Judge's hammer which he stamped to signal the commencement of the court's proceedings.

The Testimony

The first question that the Public Prosecutor asked was, "Can you recognise the accused who is present in the courtroom?"

Abhay really did not recognise Hala because she had grown weaker, darker, and looked quite different from what he saw her last and he replied, "No."

His answer created a furore in the court, Public Prosecutor was visibly disturbed and he reworded and repeated the question, "Is the accused present in the court?"

Abhay's answer still remained the same and once again he said, "No."

Abhay's answer went in favour of Hala. But as far as Hala was concerned, she took it otherwise. She was heartbroken because she thought that either Abhay had forgotten her or he had no feelings left for her. She doubted her own feelings that convinced her every time that he indeed loved her and cared for her. For a moment she thought that everything had changed and he hated her for what she had done to him and did not even want to look at her face. She asked herself, "Was Allah's intervention that sparked a love for him in her heart just an illusion?" Then she was called to the witness box in front of him and she looked at Abhay. As she stood before him, Abhay saw a broken, listless, and underconfident Khaani, and he could not believe his own eyes. He cursed himself, "How could you not recognise her?" How he wished he could run to her, take her into his arms, and say he loved her and missed her in his life. He was angry with himself for not bothering to look for her in those five years. The thought that perhaps she had to remain in prison for a few more years only because he did not appear for recording his statement made him feel guilty.

Public Prosecutor brought a pistol and a fired case and asked, "Do you recognise it?"

Abhay's eyes were glued to Khaani, he did not want to see anything else in his life except her, he kept looking at her, and he did not hear the question. The Public Prosecutor repeated the question and yet again there was no response from Abhay. The sudden murmur in the court for Abhay's behaviour was silenced by the Judge when he sternly asked him to respond to Public Prosecutor's question. That broke the connection of their eyes and hearts, and they both looked a bit embarrassed and uneasy. Khaani felt Abhay's love reach her once again and her confidence was restored. Nalini and Naveli were upset with Abhay's attention towards Hala. But Jasmina was smiling, Hala noticed that and a shy smile lit up on her lips as well.

The Public Prosecutor repeated the question, "Do you recognise it?"

Abhay replied, "No."

The Public Prosecutor was aghast and he questioned Abhay's answer, "This pistol belongs to Thakur Bodh Singh Ji Chandel, isn't it?"

Abhay replied, "Yes, but this rusted junk is unidentifiable."

The Public Prosecutor was disappointed by the way the case was shaping up, but he asked the final and the most important question, "Did the accused Hala Khan who is standing in the accused corner fire this pistol at you with an intent to kill you?" He urged Abhay to answer carefully and he deliberately restated his carefully worded question.

Abhay thought for a moment, the events of that night played in his mind, and then he answered without mincing his words, "Khaani, I mean Ms. Hala Khan is innocent. She did not fire the weapon with the intent to kill me. The pistol went off accidentally when she was taking it from my room to return the same to Thakur Baba. She could never think of killing me, she was a dedicated nurse who cared for me."

The Case Fell

He was the sole eyewitness and with his statement to the NIA Court, the case fell. There was a stunned silence in the court at the unexpected outcome of the famous case that fuelled media frenzy for over five years. Nalini, Naveli, and Sukhbir were not happy. Hala was confused. She took time to realise that Abhay's statement had completely turned the case in her favour. Suddenly Abhay made her feel small, and her self-esteem failed to measure up to his magnanimity, but her respect for him rose manifold. She slumped in the witness box and cried. But Abhay was happy, and so were Jasmina and Jehangir. After hearing the concluding arguments of the counsels, the NIA Judge made his decision but reserved the judgment to the next date a week later. Abhay left the courtroom, but he waited for Khaani to come to the police van just to meet her. Hala was the last to leave the court room and her eyes kept searching for Abhay till she reached the police van. She was relieved to see him waiting for her. She stopped for a while, their eyes met, and she had tears in her eyes, the tears of gratitude, the tears of love. Abhay came forward to meet her, however, police personnel requested him to leave her alone. He told her, "Apna Khayal Rakhna. (Take care of yourself.) I will wait for you and come again on the next date of hearing.

The Judgement

On the next date of hearing, the NIA Judge read out his carefully worded judgement in which he had discharged Hala Khan of all major charges against her, but found her guilty of negligence, and awarded her the punishment of one-year rigorous imprisonment. The judge noted that she had already spent almost five years in custody, and as such, he ordered her immediate release from prison. Hala heard the judge very carefully, and once he exonerated her of the charge of terror, she closed her eyes in silent prayers, reverence, and gratitude for Allah. Thereafter, Jasmina came and hugged her and said, "Now you can sleep with your enemy. Please come to my home after you are finally released from Tihar Jail. I will wait for you. We will go shopping at Sarojini Nagar Market together and eat gol-gappas (Street food). But where is the enemy?" After

Jasmina left, Hala started looking for Abhay, but she could not find him. She felt sad, her heart broke, and she was angry with him for not fulfilling his promise. After the necessary police formalities, she was taken back to Tihar Jail, this time, for her release. Police did not handcuff her. When she reached Tihar, she was welcomed by the inmates with the loud chants of "Khaani-Khaani". She had become Khaani after Abhay called her Khaani in the court. She had become Khaani even in the Tihar Jail after the Asma Beg incident. Every woman inmate was happy for her release. All of them wanted to celebrate her and hear her speak to them. They contributed a part of their stipends for organising a farewell for her with the permission of the jail authorities. Sunila Devi and her Kitchen team did a fairly decent job and they even invited ACP Roshni Sharma to attend Khaani's farewell. At the end of the party, Khaani was requested to say a few words to the women in her jail.

Nothing is Perfect

Khaani was a bit shy, but she said, "I am humbled by your affection. I feel and I want all of you to know that God Almighty has given every woman a lot of patience, enough courage, and sufficient strength. We have the power of love with us to make this world so very beautiful place to live. But this blessing is also a burden. Every woman is overburdened by society. I request that when some of you are released from prison, please tell your family that they have to accept that there is no such thing as perfect, especially when it comes to judging the fairer sex. Please tell them, 'When choosing a woman who works, you have to accept that she can't handle the house. If you have chosen a housewife who can take care of you and fully manage your household, you have to accept that she is not earning money. If you choose an obedient woman, you must accept that she depends on you and you must ensure her life. If you decide to be with a strong woman, you have to accept that she is tough and she has her own opinion. If you choose a beautiful woman, then you will have to accept big expenses. If you decide to be with a successful woman, you must understand that she has character and her own goals and ambitions. There are no such things as perfect. Every one of us has our own riddle, which makes us unique. Stop and think!' Always remember that hatred is the coward's revenge for being intimidated. Never be a coward, never be a victim."

All By Myself

The next day was her pre-release interview with the in-charge Women's Jail. However, in a major deviation from the protocol, DCP Jehangir Khan joined ACP Roshni Sharma for her interview. After the interview formalities and feedback, their conversation drifted into casual talks about life. Beginning the conversation, Khaani thanked DCP Jehangir Khan for everything he had done for her.

Jehangir smiled and asked, "Tell us something about your family."

Khaani smiled back and said, "I am all by myself."

"That's good. But for your age, you have suffered a lot."

"It's okay. It's okay. It's alright."

"You have such a beautiful smile, beautiful glow. No one will ever know that life has been unfair to you."

"I will be judged by society. My reputation has been ruined; character assassination will inevitably follow. I may not have any employment opportunities. That's the way things are, Sir. But that's okay. That's alright. It's important to remember that life is good."

'I must say, you are very strong."

"Sir, I have no other options."

"How do you manage that?"

"I am a great fan of Jane Kristen Marczewski, known professionally as Nightbirde. She was an American singer-songwriter. She died of cancer at the young age of 30. Her song, "It's OK" has shaped the philosophy of my life, Sir."

"Can you sing that for us?"

"Yes, I can, but now I will try to sing a few lines of "It's OK" song if you permit?"

It's OK

On Jehangir's nod, she sang, "I moved to California in the summertime,

I changed my name thinking that would change my mind.

I thought that all my problems they would stay behind.

I was stick of dynamite and it was just a matter of time, yeah,

All day, all night, now I can't hide,

Said I knew myself but I guess I lied,

It's okay, it's okay, it's okay, it's okay

If you're lost, we're all a little lost and it's alright,

It's alright, it's alright, it's alright, it's alright.

I wrote a hundred pages but I burned them all, Yeah, I burned them all.

I drove through yellow lights and don't look back at all, I don't look back at all.

Yeah, you can call me reckless, I'm a cannonball, uh, I am a cannonball,

Don't know why I take the tightrope and cry when I fall

All day, all night, now I can't hide,

Said I knew what I wanted but I guess I lied.

It's okay, it's okay, it's okay, it's okay,

If you're lost, we're all a little lost and it's alright.

Oh-oh-oh-oh, it's alright, to be lost sometimes."

Hala went into an Oblivion

It took three days for the release formalities to be completed and thereafter she was allowed to leave Tihar Jail. Before leaving the jail, she touched Dadi's feet and sought her blessings. She came out wearing the same salwar suit that Jasmina had gifted her and finally breathed free after five years. Those five years taught her life, almost ruined her life, and she had failed to fulfil the promise she made to herself at Noori. She wanted to forget and delete those five years from her life. But she could not because those years had given her Abhay, her hope, her love. After her release from prison, she directly went to Jasmina's quarter on the AIIMS premises. Jasmina had taken leave for a few days and both of them enjoyed themselves. However, one day she quietly left Jasmina's home. Given her by now much-tainted background, she did not want to endanger Jasmina's life and reputation. No one knew where she went and thereafter no one ever heard of Hala. She was later rumoured to have been killed by LeT. Hala Khan had to die for Nusrat Javed to resurface from the depths of anonymity.

THE BALUSTRADE
OF LOVE IS UNIQUE

"It's impossible," said pride. "It's risky," said experience. "It's pointless," said reason. "Give it a try," whispered the heart.

He Needed Her

Abhay got deeply involved in an intense counter-insurgency operation in the Keran sector of Jammu & Kashmir. The operation was highly successful. Seven hardcore Al Kaieda militants were killed in that operation spanning over four nights of intense gun battle; and a large cache of arms, ammunition, hi-tech communication equipment, and foreign currency was recovered in the ensuing searches. The conclusion of the operation was followed by a series of visits of the higher rung of military leadership, media briefings, and other miscellaneous formalities, and those kept Abhay continuously engaged for the next few days, thereafter. When Abhay had a breather, his first thoughts reverted to Khaani. He realised that he had missed being with her on the day of the verdict of the NIA court in her case. He felt guilty, he was sad, he was worried about her, and what bothered him more than anything else was that he had lost contact with her once again after their destiny brought them together after a lapse of five years. That was a sinking feeling. He needed her in his life. He had to find her at any cost and he immediately rushed to the Tihar Jail only to learn that no one knew where she went after her release from the prison. Even Jehangir Khan and Roshni Sharma had no idea about her whereabouts. Abhay was deeply disappointed as he returned to his unit.

The Family Opposed Abhay's Liaison with Khaani

Abhay remembered that when he had broached Baba about his love for Khaani a few years back despite everything, he was not happy. Actually, he couldn't imagine Abhay's love for a traitor. Nobody could, even Abhay was surprised at his feelings for her. Nalini and Naveli were vehemently opposed to any liaison between Abhay and Khaani. The family tried to persuade and even pressurise him to get married to a decent girl of their stature. Abhay withstood every emotional blackmail; he couldn't imagine his life without her and decided to remain a bachelor for life. As far as Abhay was concerned, it was to be Khaani or on one else in his life. The family stood their ground, and so did Abhay. As time went by, both Nalini and Naveli were married and they settled down in UK and US respectively. Initially, Baba spent a lot of time in UK and US, but later he mostly remained in India and occasionally visited Abhay. On his part, Abhay never flinched on his responsibility towards his Baba, Nalini, and Naveli. They had a lot of discussions on Khaani, but Abhay's idea of marrying a terror accused appalled Baba. The topic of Khaani had portends of unpleasantness between the father and son and to that extent, Abhay never carried those discussions beyond a point after which Baba could be hurt. He loved him more than anything else in his life. Over time, however, Baba felt that Abhay's happiness was more important to him than anything else.

Go Find Her

Those feelings were not impromptu, they were built up over time and eventually resulted in his realisation and understanding of the depth of Abhay's love for his lass. However, they were triggered when one night Abhay could not contain his deep emotions towards her. Abhay had come on a short leave, and as usual, they both were a bit happier on booze when the topic of Khaani found a reason to join them on that rainy evening. Surprisingly, Abhay was unusually quiet that day externally, but his inner realm was coaxing him to speak for his feelings. Abhay did not say a word externally, but he spoke to her and God within himself, oblivious of Baba's presence with him. He said to himself, "At the resurrection, I'll rise from death with the stain of your love. Even that time, my heart will be filled with your memories. How should I narrate my condition? How should I address this pain? O, God! Is my pain a part of my destiny? Why am I crying? My love is my worst enemy. How should I deal with it? What kind of madness is this love? What kind of pain is this love? I don't even know where my life is leading me to. Who is pulling my life towards you? My destiny is angry with me. And my happiness too! My dreams are shattered. Perhaps the tears in my eyes are markers of my unhappiness. Got memories of someone parted. I am not able to control my tears. Did we part somewhere, sometime in our past lives? Did someone snap the thread of blood between us with a sharp knife? This kind of pain is unbearable, it is crazy, and it is driving me to my death. How should I tend to the sufferings of my heart? I may get used to myself. God! My Atarangee Antarman is pleading with me to spare me this kind of punishment of love. You created this world and filled every pore of it with love. The story of love lives in every heart. The destination of love is deep, and yet unknown. The balustrade of love is unique. The heart is the habitat of love. The love roams over the skies. Why have you deprived some hearts of love? I too want it, but it only listens to the beloved." Although Abhay had spoken nothing, his face, moist eyes, and silence told the tale of his love for Khaani. In their earlier conversations, Baba was usually bemused at Abhay's recalcitrance on Khaani. He always thought that Abhay's thoughts were inconsistent, incoherent, and even illogical. But that evening, it certainly made sense to him that his son would find his happiness only in his love. There was that uncanny feeling of a past life connection. Although there is no way of knowing that, the reality of that connection in his case bore its own testimony in Abhay's tears. But was that one-sided? What if Khaani wasn't feeling the same way? Baba had realised that some justifications should be left to justify themselves. At least he felt he read Abhay's sadness that way that evening, saw some sense in his silence, and he decided to place the happiness of his son above everything. The next day Baba called him and said, "Go find her. Although I will never be able to forgive her for hurting you, I will accept her for you." Abhay wanted to find her, but he could not find a way to connect to her. It was at that juncture when DCP Jehangir Khan came to him. He found her again and lost her once again. Abhay was in those thoughts when his flight from Delhi landed at the Sheikh Ul Alam International Airport, Srinagar. It was a jerky landing and that effectively brought Abhay out of his thoughts into reality.

Nusrat Javed

Past 10 p. m. that cold night, there was a knock on the door of Abeeda Begum's hut in Keran, a border village in Neelam Valley in Pakistan Occupied Kashmir. There was no electrification in that area and the cold climate ensured that the villagers went to bed early. Only the terrorists visited the village late at night for food and shelter. It was for that reason, that the late-night knock on her door was an indication that the terrorist(s) would be hiding in her hut for the night. She silently cursed them because that meant she had to cook for them and thereafter, keep the fire burning through the night to keep them warm. But she was not worried. Both of her daughters were already abducted, probably raped, and perhaps forcefully married to foreign militants. That was the case with all the border villages in their area. As she prepared to get up, the door was knocked again. Abeeda increased the light of her lantern and opened the door. She took her time to recognise Mansoor Ahmad Khan who was the younger brother of Javed Khan, and he was accompanied by Nusrat Javed. The moment she saw her, she was worried about her safety, and she pulled her in quickly. Leave aside any hint of welcome, she cursed Javed for sending her and Mansoor for bringing beautiful Nusrat to Keran. She said, "Why have you brought Nusrat here? She is so beautiful and so young. Sometimes your beauty becomes your worst enemy. In our case, even beauty is not an issue, here every woman is only an object of abduction, rape, murder, or marriage to foreign terrorists in Afghanistan,

Pakistan, or other Muslim countries. You knew it well that our villages on the borders are a hot hub of militancy in the valley. They have forcibly taken away all young women of our village and they will take Nusrat too tomorrow."

Mansoor said, "Believe me, Abeeda Begum, we were equally worried about Nusrat, but there was no other place in this world at this time where I could have taken her for her safety. We had no time to think. Javed Bhai (Brother) and Aameena Bhabhi (Sister-in-Law) were brutally tortured and murdered just a few hours back by Amanullah Pathan for helping their daughter escape his nefarious designs on her."

Abeeda was stunned in silence, but Nusrat cried in pain and anger when she heard about the killing of her parents. Nusrat vowed to kill Amanullah, the beast. Abeeda muffled her cries by hugging her tightly and said, "Amen. I will protect you even with my blood. Allah will help you, my child. Never go out of our hut, don't even look out of the window or open the door for anyone. You should hide even if the neighbours come to look for me. Let Allah figure out our lives Beta (Child)."

Ray of Hope

Mansoor Khan offered Isha (Muslim Prayer) for their safety and left immediately thereafter leaving Nusrat with Abeeda. Nusrat thought that she had normalised her pain, but the news of the brutal killing of her parents had shocked her beyond belief and stunned her into a deafening silence. She was seething in anger but had no means to give vent to her injured feelings. Helplessness is one of the worst experiences of life and no one knew it better than Nusrat Javed. She was somewhat intrigued to find Abhay intrude her thoughts in those terrible moments of her life, and he once again had brought a bleak ray of hope in her turbulent and distressing times. She felt better, albeit very briefly, and she smiled. Life is so strange and smiles stranger than life. Nusrat smiled briefly not for him, but at the thought of Abhay killing Amanullah Pathan, all his accomplices, and slaying her pains as well. That vicious smile embraced an unimaginable quantum of pain and a bit of hope. Abeeda Khaala was observing her and her smile worried her, but she decided to keep mum on that for the time being. Nusrat hardly spoke for the next 10 days or so. She was externally quiet, but a strong storm was brewing up inside her. Khaala was worried about her. She was quite uncertain about their future, and she was struggling to discover a method in the madness of life. Her staunch belief in Allah helped her nurture a semblance of some hope in their lives. She offered regular Namaz (Prayers) for the safety and wellbeing of her young niece. But her first task was to make Nusrat speak, and her unconditional love for her encouraged her to speak to her Khaala.

THE GREAT ESCAPE

"Human mind communes with the Divinity which is the ruler of heaven and earth; mind and Divinity are one and the same. Divinity is the root origin of heaven and earth, the spiritual nature of human destiny. Itself without form, it is Divinity which nurtures things with form."

– Kanetome Yoshida

Design of Destiny

Over a period of time, Nusrat narrated her plight to her after her release from the Tihar Jail. She said, "After I left Jasmina's home, I came to my rented accommodation in Mir Haadi's house in Srinagar. When I reached there, I found that the house was deserted. It appeared as if no one had ever lived there. I went to the neighbours' house only to be told that Mir Haadi was mercilessly murdered in a broad daylight right in front of his home a few years ago. They had no clue about the whereabouts of my flatmates, Hania Saeed and Sana Khan. They were feared killed as well. I was informed that the terrorists would be following me, and soon I will meet the same fate. I was also advised to get out of the valley as soon as possible and hide in oblivion if I wanted to live. I really wanted to live, and I had firm faith in the fairness of the ways of Allah. But I could not flee for I was worried about my parents. I had to reach them and go to our village Noori. But my fate had some other plans for me and I received a message from two motorcycle-borne boys to reach a Masjid at Doda. I had no option but to follow the dictate and I reached the Masjid that night itself. Khaala, surprisingly I was strong and I had no fear whatsoever. I was, however, a bit anxious about my destiny's design on me. I had my food and went off to sleep. The next day onwards, what commenced as Islamic education for me soon turned out to be the process of radicalisation to eventually make me a Fedayeen and carry out a strike against the Kaafirs. I had neither the desire nor inclination to be one, but I had to bear that very organised and systematic, but torturous process.

Jashn (Celebration)

Meanwhile, an already twice married Maulvi Mama had cast his libidinous eyes on me and he wanted to take me in his Nikah as his third wife. I was in love with Abhay, and I had the debt to pay for what he had done for me and the way he stood for me during my worst times. I had no option but to run away. I did not know where to go, but I had to go and go sooner rather than later. But Mama denied me that option by setting my Nikah on the very next day. Allah Miya intervened for good or bad, and that very day, Amanullah reached Masjid looking for me. The first thing he did was to kill Maulvi there and then. One beast killed another beast and it seemed that I was in for bigger trouble. I was amazed at the regularity of the dramas unfolding in my life, for the worse.

I thought perhaps, Allah was still testing me. The next very moment, Amanullah Pathan, who was Rashid Bhai's assistant, pulled me roughly towards him and threw me inside his room with stern instructions to his guards to ensure that I do not leave the room. I overheard him mention some kind of Jashn (Celebrations) later that night. I must mention that despite everything going wrong for me, I was quite pampered in that room that day. I somehow had a feeling that my condition was no different from that of a sacrificial goat which is groomed just before the Halaal. (Islamic form of Slaughtering Animals, and/or Humans)

Back to Noori

I feared the worst for me and my thoughts wandered once again towards Abhay. Abhay had become a single reference point for me to bank on when I was in trouble. And that once again gave me hope and with some kind of positive energy, I offered Fajr (Type of Namaz) and Maghrib (Type of Namaz at the Sunset) Ki Namaz with utmost sincerity for Ammi-Abbu's (Mother-Father's) and my wellbeing. Immediately after the Namaz, I heard a knock on the window of the room where I was confined and detained. I was very apprehensive, but I had to answer that knock on my window. When I opened the window, I found Rahim Bhai, who was Rashid Bhai's childhood friend, standing in front of me. Without any sort of unnecessary prelude, he directly told me, "Hurry, we have to leave before someone notices us." I jumped out of the window and we quietly slipped out of the Masjid in the darkness of the night. He told me, "This Amanullah Pathan is a Haraami (rascal). He is the one who perhaps tipped the security forces about your brother visiting Noori for your Nikah with Shehzad

Mukhtar. He had cast an evil eye on you the moment he saw you for the first time when he accompanied Rashid Bhai to Noori to celebrate the last Eid before your Nikah. Remember, he gave you a diamond ring as your Eidi (A gift that is given to children by older relatives or family friends as part of the celebration of two Muslim festivals: Eid-al-Fitr and Eid-al-Adha) and how Rashid Bhai had admonished him and asked you to return the ring? Rashid Bhai was a devout Muslim and he had firm faith in Allah. He was a man of principle and he never harmed innocent people. Yes, he always attacked the Security Forces, and you know the reason for that. Unlike Rashid Bhai, Amanullah Pathan is an evil and unscrupulous man. He wanted to rape you repeatedly tonight, drug you, thereafter strap you with explosives, and dump you near the busy Laal-Chowk Police Station with a timer to explode the human bomb in the busy hours ostensibly for killing the police personnel and innocent people, but actually to get rid of you and along with you destroy the proof of his misdeeds. I will leave you with a trusted family who will take care of you and escort you to Noori at an appropriate time. I have to leave now before the needle of suspicion points at me." Rahim Bhai was killed the moment he reached Doda Masjid and buried there unceremoniously in the hours of darkness. Thereafter, began a frenetic search for me, but the terrorists could not find me. At an opportune moment which was considered safe for me to return, I was escorted to Noori. I remember, I reached home in the afternoon that day and met my Ammi- Abbu after almost five years. It was a very emotional reunion and we were very happy to be back together once again. Ammi prepared Wazwan and Nadru Yakhni (Traditional Kashmiri Food) for me and I loved it. We missed Rashid Bhai and talked a lot about him. Later, Ammi applied Almond Oil to my hair. But before that wonderful feeling of being back home could barely sink into me, a worried Mansoor Chacha (Uncle) came in quietly and informed Abbu about Amanullah heading towards their village in search of me. It was already a bit too late because when Abbu looked out of the window, he saw that Amanullah was already there and he was rushing towards our home. Abbu asked Chacha to get me out from the back door of the house and take me to you." Khaala was deeply moved by the ordeal that young Nusrat had been enduring. Her thoughts drifted towards the plight of her daughters, and she silently prayed for their wellbeing. She knew she wouldn't be able to do anything for them, but she vowed to protect Nusrat till her last breath. She kept quiet and simply hugged her for a long time.

Nusrat Remembers Abhay

Abeeda Khala with her limited resources really took good care of her. But Nusrat normally remained depressed after the death of her parents and brother. She felt bad for Rahim Bhai as well. She smiled occasionally whenever she thought of Abhay. After about six months of hiding, some sort of hopelessness was upsetting her. She sincerely felt that Abhay was her only hope and she was rather desperate to meet him, but there was no way she could do that. Moreover, she was in Pakistan and he was in India. But those nagging feelings for him still gave her hope and that to an extent countered her helplessness and loneliness. She often spoke to herself about Abhay thus, "I have that constant fear that I am never going to forget you. The way your brown eyes pierced mine or your goofy grin made my heart beat many times faster, and what sucks the most is that you were never mine, to begin with. You were my enemy who killed my brother. But I fell hopelessly in love with you. It has been more than five years and I can't forget you. In the middle of the night when everything is quiet and everyone's asleep, I thought of you. Even if I didn't realise it, you would find your way back in my memory to the point where it made me sick in my stomach and I couldn't breathe because I didn't want to live without you. It really sucks because I thought I was forgetting you and I was finally happy. And then the memory of you comes back, and I'm sitting in the corner of my hut, tears pouring down my face and my throat burns because I am screaming to the ceiling begging myself to forget you. I can't and I cry at my helplessness. My Rashid Bhai was so good, but I hated him when he often said prophetically that the young man who would kill him would be my beau. I never believed him, but you did kill him. Why did you kill someone I loved the most, Abhay? Did Allah send Rashid Bhai only to be the reason for our union? Why did you come to Noori Abhay? I could have killed you anytime when you were not fit enough to defend yourself. Why couldn't I do that? Why?"

Who is Abhay?

Abeeda felt that there was something more than what she thought was troubling Nusrat and she had noticed a certain kind of queasiness in her behaviour. She mostly did not speak, but at times she talked to herself. Once when Nusrat was in her thoughts, she asked, "Who is Abhay and how do you know him? Isn't he the Indian Army commando who killed Rashid? Where did you meet him?"

Nusrat was caught unaware, but she put a counter-question, "How do you know Abhay?"

"That means you know him."

"I mean yes, but how do you know that?"

"It is not difficult. You mentioned his name a little earlier when you were telling me about you in Doda Masjid, and you keep saying his name in your dreams. And the sparkle that I saw in your eyes the moment you uttered his name tells your story."

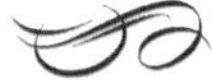

Mitti Ho Ja Mera Baccha

"Life is uncertainty, unpredictability, even irrationality, make it what it is: worthwhile, a blessing. You can see its attributes as appalling, boring, cunning, or as adventurous, beautiful, and captivating. Your choice."

– ABC of Life

Nusrat Professes Her Love for Abhay

There was no escape and hence she told her about Abhay and his family. She poured her heart out to her, but she couldn't say what she was feeling in her Antarman. She wanted to say, "Khaala, why are the memories of him emerging in my empty eyes? It seems I am dying while living my life without him. Why is my beloved not with me? Why are we living away from each other? I have heard that God lives within the heart, but what happens when the heart breaks? I feel there might be an experience there, yet unknown to me. If I don't chant Abhay, Abhay, what else should I do? I inhale and exhale, but when my inhalation meets my exhalation, I find him there. Everything turns dark there, my helplessness increases, and I have no clue of what to do. I kissed it and touched my eyes with it. You tell me, whom should I complain to? He will never be back. How should I convince my heart? I have heard that Allah is aware of the conditions of loving hearts. Time is running out and Abhay has not come back to assure me of that. I am hoping for an indication. Will there be one, Khaala? I keep saying his name because I don't know what else to do. I have been saying his name so many times that it appears that his name has become my name." However, when she was telling her about Abhay, Khaala kept observing her facial expressions which became a reflection of her inner realm and she understood the depth of her love for Abhay. She was amazed at the power of love and the fact that love could survive even in the most hopeless circumstances. She should have been worried about Nusrat's fragile future, but she felt happy for the sheer belief and hope of a young woman of finding her love someday.

Accept Reality of Life

But reality had to be accepted because that was the only way forward for them. She decided to guide Nusrat about her life. She said, "Beta, (Child) you have been convicted by a court of law. Society is not concerned about the truth. It considers you a criminal and terrorist. Nobody will trust you. No one will ever employ you. Amanullah Pathan and other terrorists are out to get you. There is hardly any hope in your life. Is that sort of life worth living? A life without purpose is equal to not living."

What Khaala was saying made a lot of sense and to that extent, Nusrat had to be strong enough to face the reality of life, and she wanted to make sense of her life ahead. She couldn't go back and the only way forward was to act, but what? She looked at her Khaala and asked, "What should I do Khaala?"

"You have two options."

"What are the options, Khaala?"

"Dishonourable option is that you die, and the honourable option is to find Abhay."

"Dying is always an option. But how do I find Abhay? That's not in my control."

"That you leave on Allah. You have to decide what exactly you want. That's something that you can always do."

Mitti Ho Ja

"Khaala, Mujhe Sirf Dil Ka Sukoon Chahiye. Mujhe Kisi Cheez Ki Itni Zaroorat Nahin Hai Jitni Iski. Mujhe Nahin Pata Mujhe Kaise Milega, Aap Mujhe Bataen. Aap Jo Kahengi, Jaisa Kahengi, Jaisa Bataengi, Main Karungi. Mujhe Sirf Dil Ka Sukoon Chahiye."

(Aunt, all I want is peace of my mind. I don't need anything else in my life. Nothing is more important than that. I don't know where will I get that from. You tell me. Whatever you say, the way you say, and whatever that be, I will do. I only need the peace of my mind.)

Abeeda asked, "Tujhe Sukoon Chahiye Beta?"

(You need the peace of mind, my child?)

Nusrat nodded her head repeatedly in affirmation and anticipation, but she did not say anything. She believed and expected that her Khaala would guide her, and she wanted to listen to her.

Abeeda took note of her desperation and measured each of the words that she spoke thereafter and continued, "Tu Apni Maye Maar De. Ye Ghinn, Galasad, Karaahat, Ye Sab Lafz Chod De Beta. Mitti Ho Ja Nusrat, Mitti Ho Ja." She looked at Nusrat's face for a long time and spoke after a long pause, "Mitti Hogi, Tere Se Jaden Footengi. Pathar To Pathar Hota Hai Beta, Mitti Se Hi Gulguden Nikaltaen Hain. Mitti Ho Ja Mera Baccha (Child), Mitti Ho Ja. Tujhe Bahut Sukoon Milega."

(To find the peace of your mind, destroy your ego, and delete such words as abhorrence scorn, and repugnance permanently from your life. Become soil and be grounded to the Earth, Soil. When you get grounded you will find your roots. The stone after all is a stone, it can't grow anything. The plants and flower buds can only grow from the soil. Become soil my child, Become soil. You will discover a lot of peace.)

Seeing an obvious confusion on Nusrat't face, Abeeda clarified, "Be optimistic about the second option and have firm faith in Allah. Jo Tha Tera Labh Jaega Kar Ke Koie Bahana Tu Jhoom. Jhoom. Jhoom. (Whatever is yours will always find ways to reach you, just have faith and relax.) When and if that option presents itself, the course suggested by me shall help you remain rooted to the ground and that will be the only way to find happiness in your life once again." That conversation between them continued till quite late at night.

Be Grounded

Nusrat couldn't sleep that night. She kept thinking of what Khaala had told her. She remembered reading T. S. Eliot, Four

Quarters, "East Coker" in her graduation course and that sounded similar to what her Khaala had told her that day. T. S. Eliot had written,

"In order to arrive at what you do not know; you must go by a way which is the way of ignorance.

In order to possess what you do not possess; you must go by the way of dispossession.

In order to arrive at what you are not; you must go through the way in which you are not.

And what you do not know is the only thing you know;

And what you do own is what you do not own;

And where you are is where you are not."

Mitti

She also remembered The Dandelion Song of Ruth B that Jasmina sang for her at AIIMS, New Delhi. She felt that her pains were like the Dandelion. The Dandelion is a symbol of hope, love, and happiness. Its yellow petals represent the sun shining on all the good deeds in your life. The black seeds of this plant are said to carry wishes for prosperity and new beginnings with them as they fly away into the sky. They can even be viewed as symbols of a free-spirited soul, of innocence, and of playfulness. Dandelions are often thought of as a symbol for strength and resilience. The Dandelion is able to survive anything from the harsh winters, pollution, drought, and being stepped on or run over by cars. They can quickly bounce back from adversity and continue to grow. Nusrat had to **become Mitti, Mitti. Dandelion.**

They were for Each Other

Abeeda with her love and wisdom continued to instil confidence in Nusrat and that saw the positive energy returning into her heart and mind. Although Abeeda was helping Nusrat find her rhythm, she was very anxious about what life had in store for this young woman. That notwithstanding, Nusrat was getting on with her life quite well, though she missed her parents and brother all the time. She took good care of her Khaala and learnt a lot of traditional cooking from her. Both of them depended upon each other for whatever happiness they derived from those dire circumstances and limited resources. Life is like that only. Nusrat followed the Tiharian (Tihar Jail) Wisdom on life that said, "Ya Toh Annian Hi Chaleli." (Life moves as it wants to.)

Cloud and Rain

"Let me, O let me bathe my soul in colours; let me swallow the sunset and drink the rainbow."

– Khalil Gibran

Rains Brought Her Memories

In order to distract himself from a continuous rill of thoughts of Khaani, Colonel Abhay Pratap Singh found an escape route through excessive work. His unit was deeply involved in anti-militancy operations in Kashmir Valley. That was the time of the year when it was raining incessantly in the valley. Those were the ideal conditions for military operations. Despite his complete involvement in the counterinsurgency operations, Khaani continued to sneak into his mind space in some way or the other. Till such time he had met her, rains represented only a suitable condition to strike terrorists on both sides of the line of control. However, after meeting her, he felt that there was much more to the cloud and rain for they invariably brought her memories for him. There was an unmissable link. He would keenly observe the cloud formations and make mental cloud images of men and women in love. He was happy when he pictured Khaani with him in those images. He remembered reading some erotic stuff about cloud and rain in Chinese mythology a few years ago. He remembered vaguely that in ancient times, people often used cloud and rain to describe things between men and women. For example, words such as turning the cloud over the rain were all imaginative. It is not difficult to find that when ancient literati and writers mentioned the matter of men and women, they would use "cloud rain" instead, which is an implicit expression. In fact, the reason why "cloud rain" is used is because of a Chinese mythological story about, "Wushan Goddess prospering clouds and sowing rain."

The Story of Cloud and Rain

The saying that "Wushan Yunyu" became a matter of lingering love between men and women was first seen in ancient texts such as Chu Ci "Gao Tang Fu" and "Goddess Fu". The story is that when King Chu Xiang and Song Yu visited Yunmengtai together, Song Yu said, "The former king, that is, King Chu Huai once visited this place, and fell asleep when he was tired of playing. Then he dreamed of a beautiful person. A charming woman, she claimed to be the daughter of Wushan, willing to give her pillows and mats to the king of Chu. It is the third part of "Gao Tang Fu" that contains the story of the matters of men and women. The ancients called intercourse as "things that go through the clouds and rain." The protagonist of this myth is Yaoji. She never fell in love before her death, and she yearns for love very much.

Gao Tang Fu encourages King Xiang to meet the Goddess, hoping to bring happiness to the country and individuals by having sex with the Goddess. The purpose is completely consistent with the cultural concept of the above-mentioned religious mythology. Of course, "cloud rain" does not only mean weather phenomena and men and women. There are many interpretations of this word in ancient times, but with the evolution and the update of the literature, people gradually accepted the expression of this meaning. So, what does "cloud rain" mean? Let's take a look.

One day, the handsome King Xiang of Chu passed by the mountain of Gao Tang, and Yaoji was attracted by the King Xiang of Chu. So, when the King fell asleep, Yaoji appeared in his dream. She told him that she was the Goddess of Wushan's cloud and rain and she was in love with him. They made love and later the stars shining in the night sky, heard the sound of the jade pendant of the Goddess, and enjoyed the fragrance on the body of the Earth after a cloud and rain. Later, "Wushan Yunyu" became synonymous with male and female love. Intercourse is also known as "Yunyu."

Symbols of Hope and Happiness

Although his memories brought a smile to his face, he did not only see cloud and rain that way. He attached spiritual dimensions to cloud and rain. They complement each other and are made for each other for eternity. He always thought of them as man and woman in love and their union is highly desirable for the nourishment of Nature. A Nimbus Cloud is their abode. God has made cloud and rain to love and spread happiness. In their case, happiness on the Earth is only possible when rain leaves her cloud leaving him empty. She falls on Earth, flows through streams, channels, and rivers, nourishes nature, flowers bloom, and birds sing for her before she finally merges with the oceans. Oceans send her back to Nimbus Cloud perhaps as his bride. They meet again, fall in love again, but don't recognise each other. That doesn't matter because they find love and feel the unbroken bond of their previous lives. At the pinnacle of their love, the rain falls once again and spreads happiness to all but her own cloud. The endless cycle of their union and separation is kind of knowing each other by not knowing. Only love knows or Cloud and Rain know or not know. He often wondered whether clouds bring rains or rains bring clouds, but they persuade the Sun to bring the rainbow. Abhay always thought of "Cloud Rain" as a symbol of happiness and hope and he genuinely felt that Khaani would unite with him sooner or later as rain unites with the cloud.

Let's Prepare for Rains

While he was still in his morning musing against the backdrop of falling rain, Apple Music played a beautiful rain song, "Let's prepare for rains", sung by Jose and Hilda Feliciano. The lyrics were as under: -

Listen to the pouring rain; Listen to it pour,

And with every drop of rain; You know I love you more,

Let it rain all night long; Let my love for you go strong.

As long as we're together; Who cares about the weather?

Listen to the falling rain; Listen to it fall.

And with every drop of rain, I can hear you call,

Call my name right and loud, I can hear above the clouds,

And I'm here among the puddles, You and I together huddle.

Listen to the falling rain, Listen to the rain.

It's raining. It's pouring; The old man is snoring,

Went to bed, and bumped his head. He couldn't get up in the morning.

Listen to the falling rain, Listen to it all,

And with every drop of rain, I can hear you call,

Call my name right out loud, I can hear above the clouds,

And I'm here among the puddles, You and I together huddle.

Mystic Experience

Now that was a good number, but Abhay had some sort of mystic experience while listening to the lovely song. When the line of hearing above the cloud was playing, he remembered calling Khaani's name loud from above the clouds during many of his high-altitude parachute jumps in the past. Was she calling him from above the clouds? Was he in the puddles of tears in huddle with immense pain? Why were they separated? Who died and when? Those were some of the questions he was hearing from within and for which he had no answers. But more intriguing were the flashes he saw when the song was playing the death of the old man. He saw him holding Khaani tightly in his arms while she suffered some sort of seizure, and he was almost shouting in desperation, "Sarloo, is it death? I won't let you go, please don't go." She did not respond; she was just looking at him with her eyes wide open, trying to say something to him, but couldn't. He distinctly remembered seeing Khaani's face, but he was calling her Sarloo. Who is Sarloo? Who is Khaani? He was disturbed. When that confusion became too much for him to bear, he shook his head and proceeded to a forward post to act on a piece of actionable information regarding the terrorists. The operation fanned out as planned and his commandos neutralised two dreaded hardcore terrorists.

Dreams Travel Time

"Trust in dreams, for in them is hidden the gate to eternity."

– Khalil Gibran

Dreams are Children of Night

While returning late that night, the lyrics of the song and the flashes of the mystic memories kept playing in his mind. He felt that ordinary experiences could be expressed easily in conventional language. The rub lies with the mystic's experience when the consciousness undergoes a change. Language can't keep pace with rapidly changing awareness. He was experiencing a new, vast, and deep way of experiencing, seeing, knowing, and contacting. He needed to adopt a much more subtle, holistic, and organic interpretation of some parts of his understanding of his feelings for her. To give expression in words to the glimpse of such a reality becomes difficult. He gave up those intense feelings, and his thoughts slipped towards his dreams. He remembered that he had not seen any of his dreams for the past almost a year. He had realised that his dreams were not only quite similar, but they also had a pattern about them. Every time he had a dream, he met Khaani.

The last time he had a dream was just before he met her in the NIA court. The long gap between his dreams indicated to him that the possibility of their meeting was waning. That was quite disappointing because it could be true as well. But he still wanted to hang on to the thin ray of hope of finding her yet again. In fact, whenever he felt like losing hope about meeting her, she would always manage to invade his thoughts in one way or the other. He was quite convinced that his dreams had some connections with his past life. They had some meaning. But what? There is a reference to the possibility of 'buying' another's conception dream in a popular Korean Drama series that he saw and which concluded recently. A dream is in itself unreal, then to have a conception dream – that foretells a pregnancy or birth of a baby, its gender, and/or its destiny – and further transact that dream as a good omen, is even more surreal. Nevertheless, looking at some mythologies, particularly concerning conception, reveals a treasure trove of interesting scenarios and stories. Greek mythology is populated with several Gods of dreams, the most well-known being Morpheus, who is said to take any shape or form in a dream. Dreams are referred to as 'children of the night' – they could be born of one's subconscious, imagination, and experience, or they could be divine prophesies. His own dreams were giving him a strong indication of some bonds of the past life between Khaani and him. He was very confident and optimistic that their meeting was a design of destiny, and their union was inevitable.

A Brave Drop of Water

As a lucky coincidence, he thought of dreams, and he had one that night. It was actually in the early morning hours.

The special thing about that dream was that he did not only see a glimpse of the beautiful lady, but he saw her clearly. She was Khaani. The other thing peculiar to that dream was that he saw the other two ladies were talking to the dusky beauty, and he vaguely remembered their conversation. But the most exciting thing was that he talked to Khaani for the first time ever in his dream and remembered the conversation between them quite clearly. The dream began with some philosophical conversations between the three ladies. They were looking at Khaani who was sitting at some distance by the side of a stream of crystal-clear water. The Dusky Beauty said, "Saral is a brave drop of water who after meeting the ocean is all set to again meet Rahul in her third light cone, that is this life; Picture this: "Saral sat gazing at the little stream in front of her. It seemed to be dancing as it tumbled over little rocks and stones on its way. It never got tired of flowing. It was not flowing because someone asked it to, but because it was in its nature. Though separate, this stream belonged to the ocean. Every drop flowing in it had emerged from the ocean and would eventually return to it. And along its journey, it was the reason for many flowers blossoming, many birds quenching their thirst, many hearts rejoicing in its beauty, many colourful fish swimming … it was the longing of the stream to merge into the ocean that made it flow. Love is the basis of its existence. And between the longing and the love, life flourished". She paused for a moment and further said – "When a drop feels connected to the ocean, it feels the strength of the ocean. This is subtle strength. The strength in a mind that feels connected to creation, the strength in a mind that is in the present moment, which is the field of all possibilities." At that juncture, one of the other two ladies intervened and added,

"Saral is such a delicate balance of strength with serenity, of sensitivity and sensibility, of beauty and brilliance, of courage and compassion, so ethereal yet approachable in subtlety. The more you know her, you cannot but love her. The real strength of mind that is unfazed by negativity and adversities, and full of faith and confidence is a blessing. Saral is a blessing of such a mind".

You Left me Alone

He was very confused. He did not understand much of what was happening in the dream. Suddenly, the three ladies disappeared and he found him conversing with Khaani.

He asked,"Tu Oopar Kya Kar Rahi Thi. Tu Mujhe Chod Ke Kahan Gayi Thi."

(Why did you leave me alone? What were you doing up and beyond the clouds?)

She replied, "Kuch Kisse Khatam Karne The Rahul, Wahi Karne Gayi Thi."

(I went up to end some affairs of my life.)

"Kaun Se Kisse? Tu Mujhe Chod Ke Toh Nahin Chali Jaegi?"

(What affairs are you talking about and why you had to leave me alone to suffer in separation? Please promise, you will never leave me alone.)

"Nahin, Kabhi Bhi Nahin. Kisse Khatum Hote Hain, Daastane Nahin. Wo Toh Amar Ho Jaati Hain."

(I promise, I will never leave you alone ever. Affairs end, not stories. Our story transacts time.)

"Main Pooch Raha Hun, Mushkil Mushkil Baten Kar Rahi Hai. Jo Pooch Raha Hun Uska Jawab De. Tu Mujhe Chod Ke Toh Nahin Chali Jaegi?"

(I am asking you something. Why are you complicating it? Please answer what I am asking you. Hope you will not leave me alone ever again?)

"Nahin, Kabhi Bhi Nahin. Chod Ke Toh Tu Mujhe Chala Gaya Tha. Kahan Chala Gaya Tha? Ab Mujhse Pakka Vada Kar Kahin Nahin Jaega."

(No, never. I did not leave you alone. You had left me alone. Where did you go? Promise, you will never leave me alone ever again.)

"Kahin Nahin Jaunga, Vada, Pakka Vada. Ek Baat Batun, Tu Ek Kaam Karna, Tu Mujhe Janzeer Se Baandh Dena. Mujhe Baandh Kar Apni Ankhon Ke Saamne Rakh Lena. Fir Main Kahin Bhi Nahin Jaunga."

(I will never leave you alone, promise, God promise. Do one thing, tie me up with a chain and keep me in front of your eyes forever. Then, I won't be able to go.)

"Haan Ye Hi Karna Padega. Par Kuch Janzeeren Paon Mein Nahin Baandhi Jati, Dil Mein Padti Hain. Jaise Tune Mere Dil Mein Dal Di Hai Ek Janzeer. Mein Kahin Nahin Ja Sakti Tujhe Chod Kar, Bandh Gayi Hun Main Tere Saath. Vaise Hi Main Ek Janzeer Tere Dil Mein Daal Dungi, Tu Bhi Kahin Nahin Ja Sakega."

(I think I will do that. But some chains are not tied to the feet, they have to be put through the heart. Like you have put one through my heart. I am permanently bound to you and I cannot go away from you ever. I will also put one chain through your heart so that you are not able to go leaving me alone.)

"Tu Bahut Pyaari Hai."

(You are very sweet.)

Rahul and Saral

Abhay woke up feeling fresh and happy from the dream. His happiness stemmed from his strong conviction that after the dream, his meeting with Khaani was imminent and that they would be meeting soon. But he was thoroughly confused as well. There were more questions than answers that were staring him in his face once again. Who were those three ladies in conversation about Saral? Who is Saral? Is Saral his Khaani? Why did she address him, Rahul? Why was the conversation between them so natural and intimate? Who left whom? Why? When? For whom? Who is Rahul? How are Rahul and Saral connected to Khaani and him? Was there a past-life connection? When he was battling such questions, he was informed by his buddy that there was someone who wanted to see him urgently. Abhay called him in. He was Akhtar, his trusted informer and he had some vital and actionable intelligence input for him. Abhay immediately gave a warning order for his team to prepare for the operation and he rushed to his controlling headquarters. Abhay along with his team crossed the line of control at the last light that day for a cross-border mission. That night it was raining heavily. That was a good omen and that kind of weather was suitable for operations. That was also an indication of finding Khaani.

Terrorists Came for Her

There was a mild storm in Keran village and it was raining non-stop that night. Khaala's roof was leaking and water was coming in through the doors and windows as well. She asked Nusrat to close both the windows properly while she put a bucket under to collect water leaking through the roof. Thereafter, they had food and tried to sleep. At around 11:00 p. m. there was a loud knock on the door. Khaala's worst fears appeared to have come true. She woke up Nusrat, asked her to flee through the window, and save herself. Meanwhile, Khaala raised the wick of the lantern and proceeded to open the door. When Nusrat opened the window, a strong gush of wind and rain water lashed at her face, she saw terrorists outside the window, and she immediately closed the window. She realised that they were trapped and the fear of the unknown gripped her. On the other hand, before Khaala could reach the door, it was broken open, and Amanullah Pathan barged in. He shoved her aside, straight way headed towards Nusrat, and she knew that was the end game. He shouted at Khaala and said, "You were hiding her for so long. You will be punished."

Khaala replied, "Let Allah decide whom to punish."

Amanullah was very angry, he pointed his gun towards her and said, "Kalma Padh Le."

(Say your prayer before I kill you.)

Nusrat was very scared and she pleaded, "No, please don't do that."

He laughed viciously and said, "You come in my Nikah, and the old woman will live."

"Amanullah Bhai", she could only say before he howled, "I am not your brother. Rashid was a fool. I was never loyal to him. Had he not been killed by that Army man; I had the plans to eliminate him and marry you there and then at Noori on the day of your Nikah."

"You traitor".

Abhay Rescues Khaani

"Shut up", he shouted and as he tried to grab her, a bullet pierced through his temple killing him on the spot. Simultaneously, there was an automatic fire outside which accounted for his accomplishes. It took less than a minute for commandos to kill Amanullah, and five other terrorists who accompanied him, and the game was over before it began. The events unfolded so fast that before Nusrat could understand, Abhay walked in, the storm relented, the rains stopped, and in a reflex action she clung to Abhay. Their heartbeats merged into each other, both heard them clearly, felt them beat harder and faster, and those moments froze for them forever. Unlike that of their first at the Maggie Point in Mussoorie, this time they embraced each other for a very long time. Their heartbeats were singing the song of their souls. That was only the second time they embraced each other, but it was so natural as if they had known each other for ages. Those were the encounters of souls and souls were laughing uncontrollably. Abhay tried to slowly separate her, but she wouldn't let him go and said, "Mujhe Chod Kar Kahan Chale Gaye The?" (Why did you leave me alone?) Abhay immediately realised and he was surprised that she had said the same words in his dream of the last night. Abhay took control of his emotions and got down to complete post-operation formalities like taking stock of captured weapons, ammunition, communication equipment, and identification. Having completed their work, the commandos finally exfiltrated into India at 4:00 a. m. the next morning. Abhay dropped Abeeda and Nusrat at the home of their trusted relatives and assured them that they would soon be settled suitably. When he was leaving Nusrat thanked him and said, "Nusrat is my name, and not Hala, and I am forever your Khaani"

Abhay was not surprised, but he said, "You need to tell me a lot of truth."

"Yes, I will."

Truth Comes in Pieces

At that point, Khaala came in and said, "The truth comes in pieces, pieces you have to put together, in order to see the big picture. But the need of the hour is that you take your Nusrat to a place of safety to save her life. Her parents have been killed by Amanullah; you had killed her brother. She is an orphan and she has been punished a lot by life at her tender age."

Abhay exclaimed, "Rashid, Rashid Javed, brother of Nusrat Javed?!" A thought flashed through his mind and he remembered every word that Rashid had said that day. And he had definitely told him to take care of his kid sister. Before he died, he had told him, "Don't harm my kid sister. Always protect her. If any harm came her way because of my deeds, God will never forgive you." He vaguely remembered Rashid calling her Nusrat. He controlled the flow of his thoughts and further said, "Please be rest assured, I will take care of everything."

Task Taken is Task Done

Abhay was aware that post that major cross-border operation, he would be busy for the next seven days or so with the management of numerous visits and media. Accordingly, he tasked Sukhbir to arrange to settle Khaala at Noori to look after the property and apple orchards of Nusrat Javed, and personally escort Nusrat to his home in Mussoorie. He requested Baba to allow her to stay in their home. Nusrat had to go by that decision because she loved him and had no other option left in her life for the time being. Reclaiming the lost trust was a humongous task and Nusrat had to take and win that challenge. Losing that would mean losing her life. No words were exchanged between them for words without the accompanying action would have become frivolous. Abhay only told her that "The task taken is a task done." And Nusrat interpreted those words in a manner that her inner realm would understand.

More Lies

When Abhay informed Baba about Nusrat, his opening lines were, "How many more lies will she tell all of us? I am not happy with the idea of her coming home." Abhay was aware of that, but he knew that Baba would respect his feelings for her. Nalini and Naveli were most certainly not comfortable with that idea and more than that they were worried about the safety of both Baba and Abhay. Nalini felt that Abhay's love for a terrorist had indeed put their reputation in society at stake. Abhay loved Nusrat and he knew that the reputation of love was much above societal acceptance. He was happy being an Army man because he knew that his love would not be judged there. He was happier for his belief that Nusrat will definitely dent the loneliness of Baba and take care of him and his home. He prayed for Nusrat to survive the indifference and indignity that awaited her in their home. The way to happiness passed through the paths of trust and love, and fortunately, Nusrat Javed had no other option but to walk that path.

KHAANI COMES HOME

Unattended Emotions

Baba had got the same room done up for her where she had stayed earlier, but he was not comfortable with the idea of Hala or Khaani or Nusrat or whatever was her name living in their house, especially after what she had done to them. She did not only hurt Abhay but also betrayed their trust big time. He was quite appalled at the thought of living with a terrorist in their house where patriotic fervour was the order of the day and huge respect for soldiering was a norm. He was aware that despite everything, his son loved her and he had no option but to allow her to stay with him. He tried to remain positive to the extent possible, however, the internal conflict between his love for Abhay and hate for Nusrat took its toll on his already deteriorating health, and his blood pressure (BP) and sugar levels shot up. Life was taxing Baba. He had become frail, but he managed to put up a brave front for Naveli, Nalini, and Abhay. Ever since the demise of Thakuraien Sahiba

Sangeeta Devi Ji, his emotions remained unattended and he was deprived of the intimate care and give of a woman for a long time. He had learnt to live with the tastelessness of his life. When Nalini and Naveli grew up, they managed to put together some semblances of emotional support and adequate care for him, and that helped him catch up with life to a great extent. After Nalini and Naveli got married, he was once again staring at a long tunnel of the looming void in his life. This time Baba was coping up well, but age was catching up with him, and the unpleasant Khaani episode really troubled him. That notwithstanding, he took special care to look good to Abhay because he did not want to burden him with emotional stress when he was involved in a very intense anti-militancy operation in Kashmir Valley. However, the news of Nusrat coming to live with him put him under pressure once again. Abhay was aware that even though Baba tried to remain upbeat in life, he was unwell, and the deficiency of affection and emotional support was affecting him adversely. Abhay was keen to protect the aura of his father but that couldn't be ensured in the third-party care of his helpers at home. For some reason, however, he felt that Nusrat shall surely make a difference and bring about a positive change in his otherwise insipid life. He did not know why, but he was confident that Nusrat was right for him. Whether reposing so much faith in Nusra would be the right decision, only time would say. As of now, he knew that Baba was not happy. He had only respected his love for his son.

Class Difference

When Sukhbir brought her home, Baba was sitting in lawns, and observing the sun set in the backdrop of the orangish-red sky. Nusrat glanced through the deserted garden as she went to wish him, he deliberately did not notice, and in fact, he simply ignored her. Nusrat had seen the worst in life, she anticipated that reaction, and to that extent, Baba's indifference towards her was on the expected lines only. Though she felt humiliated, she managed to hold her emotions well. It was an irony of sorts that she was not welcome in the same home which eventually would be hers. Maali Kaka's wife (Gardener Uncle's wife) escorted her in. When she entered the home, it looked disheveled and it wore an almost deserted look. She felt and absorbed the unhappiness of that once happy home. She was led into the very same room where she had stayed earlier. The room said the same sad story and it called for a lot of care. Perhaps, it bore the anger that the family nursed against her. She was obviously not happy, she couldn't sleep that night, and her thoughts hopped aimlessly from one topic to another. She was overthinking. She felt that between the place that she came from and this home, there was a class difference, and her dark period of the past six years only widened the gap. Baba's indifference that evening triggered the thought, that struck her hard and combined with her horrible experiences of the past six years together pushed her to once again talk to her diary that night. She wrote, "Class Difference ... Ek Bahaut Bada difference Hota Hai ... Lakh Koshish Ke Bawajood Barsaat Mein Jagah Jagah Ug Aane Wali Khumgiyon Ki Tarah Hota Hai ... Wahaan Pe Taqleef Pahunchata Hai ... Jahaan Yeh Umeed Bhi Nahin Hoti ... Kanta Ban Kar Chubta Hai Lekin Nazar Nahin Aata ... Aabla Bankar Dukhta Hai Lekin Dikhta Nahin Hai. Zindagi Mein Bahot Dafaa Bahot Se compromises Kiye Hain Maine ...Compromises, Qurbaaniyaan. Baaz Dafaa Toh Lagta Hai Hamare Liye Zindagi ... Sirf Aediyaan

Ragadne Ka Naam hai … Chhoti Chhoti Khushiyon Ke Liye … Zindagi Ki Buniyaadi Zarooiyaat Ke Liye … Har Cheez Ke Liye Tarasna Padta Hai … Sisakna Padta Hai … Main Sochti Hoon … Allah Talah Ne Hamaari Zindagi Itni Mushkil Kyon Bana Di Hai. Main Baar Baar Yehi Sochti Hoon … Yehi Poochhti Rahti Hoon Lekin Jawab … Jawab Kahin Se Nahin Miltaa … Aaj Main Bahot Thak Gai Hoon … Aur Patanahi … Baaz Dafaa Aesa Kyon Hota Hai … Ki Aap Thak Jaate Hain … Haalaan Ki Aapne Na Toh Jismani Mashaqat Kee Hoti hai … Aur Nahi Hi … Zehnee …Phir Bhi Zindagi Bekaar Lagti Hai … Aur Apna Wajood … Apna Wajood Bojh Lagtaa Hai …Zindagi Mein Aane Waali Har Musibat Par … Main Soocha Karti Thi Ki Shayad …Yeh Aakhiri Musibat Ho Aur Isse Badi Musibat Mujh Par Nahin Aa Sakti … Lekin Who Sab Theek Nahin Tha … Jitnee Zillat Aaj Maine Mehsoos Ki Hai Dobara Kabhi Nahin Kar Paungee."

(The class difference is a huge difference. Despite our best efforts to deny its existence, it grows as the wild grass grows everywhere during rains. It hurts us on every front, and from the most unexpected quarters. It pricks us like a thorn but we don't see it, it is like an ulcer that pains but we can't see it. I have made many compromises many times in my life; many sacrifices. At times it appears that life is only an ongoing struggle for me. I have to struggle, I have to shed tears for the smallest of the joys, cry for the bare minimum necessities, for every small thing in my life. I often think why has God made our lives so difficult? I think that all the time, I ask the same question again and again, but answer, I don't get any answer. Today, I am very tired. I don't know why am I tired. Why do we feel tired when we have not done any physical or emotional exercise? Life appears to be useless and we are forced to carry the burden of our existence. My sufferings don't seem to end and with every problem that plagues my life, I think that there can be no bigger problem than that and perhaps that would be my last struggle. But that was not to be. Everything was not right, and I felt that I won't be able to tolerate the kind of humiliation that I faced today.)

It was Time to Become Soil

Thereafter, the first question that came to her mind was, "Why did Abhay send her there?" At that very moment, a strange smile erupted on her lips and she spoke to herself, "Ab Mitti Ban Jane Ka Waqt Aa Gaya Hai, Nusrat." Time has certainly come to become soil, and take the test of life without any traces of ego, abhorrence, growling, and repugnance because flower buds only grow from the soil and not from the stones. She had to grow the buds of happiness and love in Baba's heart and his beautiful home. She was too naive to even imagine, and she did not bother to understand what would that mean to Baba, Nalini, Naveli, Abhay, and their home. She had to do her best. Her thoughts traced her eyes to a fairly large portrait of Thakuraien Sahiba Sangeeta Devi Ji in the centre of the house. She was smiling and Nusrat felt her speak to her, "Mitti Ho Ja Beta. I love you. Make this place a loving home again. You can do it, and you will do it. When and if life tests you unfairly, look at me and never give up." Nusrat meant "Victory", she was meant to conquer, and life was rightly calling her to win her over. Way to victory never went through the skies, it was rooted in the ground. And the process of becoming "Mitti" began from the moment she saw Baba watching the setting of the sun in a pall of gloom.

Not Seen Not Heard

When she started, the first thing that she ensured was that she was not seen and not heard by Baba. She began by taking care of him; the right diet, medicines on time, appropriate combination of dresses for him; everything from behind the scene. Her dedicated efforts bore fruits, and all-around improvements marked her presence slowly, but steadily. The house became home, home décor intimate, and the garden greener. Baba was becoming better and he was finding his aristocratic attitude back. He noticed the positive changes, took his time, and acknowledged her devoted efforts. He knew she would come to his room late in the night just to have a look at him, even adjust the night comforters, and slowly exit taking care not to disturb him. That had become her daily routine. The old charm of the bungalow was returning with all the affection and grace of the young woman. He no longer wanted to eat alone in his room and ate every meal at the well-laid dining table. The food that Nusrat prepared was amazing. He no longer stayed glued to the television, he preferred to go for long walks, and played golf twice a week instead. He started meeting his friends all over again, home smiled with the loud laughter of old buddies, and his loneliness began to diminish gradually. He knew that Nusrat was ushering in those positive changes in his life. She cared for all and there was a kind of happiness in the home that he had never witnessed after the untimely demise of Sangeeta Devi Ji. Nusrat had a natural charm that made her acceptable and lovable to all. Baba was aware that she did not want to be seen by him, but her loving care showed her presence in every nook and corner of his home. When everyone rested, she helped Dalpat Singh Ji (Maali Kaka) in the garden. She was a child of nature and she was very happy tending to the plants and blooming flowers. Dalpat Singh had felt a lot of affection for Abhay when as a five-year-old he first came to Niti. He was surprised that he had the same feelings for Nusrat as well. Whenever she laughed, it appeared that the whole home laughed with her. But she kept herself behind the scenes only and managed everything so very efficiently. Baba was forgetting his bitterness and he looked for opportunities to have a glimpse of her. He wanted to sit with her, talk to her, and shower his affection upon her. He was proud of Abhay's choice. She drew her strength in her love for Abhay. She was aware that she was making a place in Baba's heart. The gestures of his concerns and affection reached her heart and bolstered her confidence in herself after almost six years in her life.

SHE WAS NOT A TERRORIST

There is one thing alone that stands the brunt of life throughout its course: a quiet conscience.

The Experience was Empowering and Enriching

One day, Abhay informed her that Nalini and Naveli were visiting home with their families and he cautioned her about the newer and bigger challenges ahead for her. Nusrat had no problems with challenges. She had become "Mitti" and tasted the merits of being grounded. Finally, the day arrived when Nalini and Naveli came home, nursing all sorts of apprehensions, biases, and prejudices against Nusrat. Baba welcomed them wholeheartedly and brought them in. Nusrat was standing in a far corner and she wished them from there. Both of them gave her a scornful look, ignored her, and did not acknowledge her greetings. Baba noticed that and he did not appreciate their behaviour, but he preferred to keep quiet and allow them to make their own opinion about her in the due course of time. But he was very happy to meet them after a long time. He was especially thrilled to meet his grandkids.

Nalini and Naveli did not fail to notice the positive changes. The home was meticulously maintained, things were definitely more organised, intimate care and affection were palpable, and above all Baba was happy. Nusrat remained invisible, but a paradigm shift in the happiness of their home was amply apparent. Their mother's photo in the centre of the home appeared to be smiling more. Biases started breaking, prejudices crumbling, and that nagging distrust and anger, fuelled by her hurting Abhay, started easing into growing affection for her. Nusrat felt the affection and the accompanying indicators of acceptance reach her. She was happy, but she did not lower her stance a wee bit. She had understood that goodness costs, but it earned respect for her, and that had mitigated the cost of goodness to a great extent. And if the cost was of her becoming "Mitti", she was loving it because the egoless living was scaling the horizons of her happiness. The whole experience was certainly empowering and it enriched her life. She overcame the pains of her past.

She was Not a Terrorist

The whole family wanted to be with her, see her, talk to her, but she by then had become accustomed to working from behind the scenes only and she was hardly seen and hardly heard. However, when everyone rested, she played with the kids in the afternoons. Kids loved her, she laughed with them, and everyone loved her carefree and hearty laugh. Nalini and Naveli had begun to trust her and again, wanted her to be part of the family, but they did not know how to approach her for that. Things worked out when the kids wanted to be with her all the time. Both the brothers-in-law, in connivance with Abhay, seized the opportunity to persuade her and eased her into the folds of the family. That was a huge gesture and when Baba placed his hand on her head to bless her, she was overwhelmed by her emotions and cried her heart out. Nalini and Naveli hugged her and calmed her down. After about a month, all of them left. They were happy to leave Baba in the caring company of Nusrat. That night she spoke to Abhay and allowed her tears to flow freely. Those were the tears of joy, the joy of accomplishment of a mission that was nearly impossible. She had finally found acceptance, without being judged or strings attached to her past. She had exonerated herself that day of being considered a terrorist, or a traitor. She found her free spirits. She was a Mitti which was so pure.

Life is a Congregation of Strange Things

That night she gave a vent to her pent-up emotions and poured her heart out to Abhay on the phone, "Zindgi Bahot Si Ajeeb Baton Ka Majmooha Hai, Ajeeb Bataen, Ittefaqaat, Baa Dafaa Smajh Nahi Aati. Agar Isko Khabhie Ek Jumle Mein define Karna Pade Toh Woh Kya Hoga? "Zindgi Gulzaar Hai", Jaise Tum Usko Kehte Ho. Kaie Saal Pehle, Main Apni Zindagi Mein Aane Wali Har Takleef Par Allah Talah Ko Ilzaam Diya Karti Thi – Shikayaton Ka Ek Dher Tha Jo Main Har Waqt Uske Saamne Laga Diya Karti Thi. Mujhe Hamesha Is Cheez Ka Afsos Rehega Ki Main Allah Ko Galat Samajhti Thi. Uski Taqat Aur Hiqmat Ke Bare Mein Galat Andaaz Lagati Thi. Muhje Lagta Tha Ki Allah Mujhse Pyaar Nahi Karta Haalanki Allah Toh Sab Se Pyaar Karta Hai. Woh Nematen Bhi Deta Hai Aur Aazmaata Bhi Hai. Par Ye Baat Pata Nahin Zaldi Samajh Kyun Nahi Aati. Zindagi Abhi Khtam Nahi Hui, Bas Faraq Ye Hai Ki Ab Meri diary Mein Allah Se Shikve Kam Ho Gaye Hain. Maine Un Cheezon Par Raazi Hona Sheekh

Liya Hai Jo Woh Mujhe Deta Hai Aur Un Cheezon Ki Talaash Chod Di Hai Jo Na Haasil Hain."

(Life is a congregation of strange things; strange things, coincidences, surprises. It is impossible to understand it. If you have to describe it in one line what will that be? "Life is a paradise of happiness", as you would say. Some years back, I blamed God for every difficulty that I encountered. Every time I was in trouble, I would dump a big load of my complaints before him. I will forever regret that I thought God was wrong. I miscalculated his strengths and kindness all the time. I felt that God did not love me, though I am aware that God loves everyone. He grants us successes as well as fresh challenges. Why couldn't I comprehend that simple thing with natural ease? Life is still going on in the same way, but the only difference is that I have minimised complaining to God. I have learnt to live with everything that God gives me, and stopped the quest for those which are not in my control.)

Superb Chemistry

Abhay heard her patiently, understood her emotional state, and complimented her for winning every heart in his home. He was proud of her for it was only she who could do that improbable task. She had built up an unenviable rapport with Baba and his friends. She was his best friend and often accompanied him for long walks. She cared for him unconditionally but never made him feel dependent on her. They played ludo, had long chats, and watched Pakistani Dramas on YouTube. They were so much into each other that many a time she almost forgot to talk to Abhay. She had become Baba's favourite child, she cared for him as if he was her child, and at times he lovingly called her Maa. (Mother). But one question that bothered him was as to why did she want to kill Abhay? Fearing he might hurt her; he did not want to ask her that. But he wanted to know, and perhaps she thought that the time was ripe to tell Baba about it and cement their relationship on firmer ground.

THE STORY OF NUSRAT JAVED

"I'm selfish, impatient, and a little insecure. I make mistakes, I am out of control and at times hard to handle. But if you can't handle me at my worst, then you sure as hell don't deserve me at my best."

– Marilyn Monroe

The Long Walk

One pleasant morning there was a nip in the air and they went for a long walk. After they had walked for approximately two km, it suddenly started raining and they had to take shelter under a shed near Maggie Point. She remembered that she had come there with Abhay in the morning of the day she shot him, and in a rare coincidence, it was raining the same way on that day also. That memory disturbed her a bit, and though she tried to appear normal, Baba noticed her unease, but he said nothing. They both enjoyed the hot Maggie noodles and relished masala omelettes. She was happy to see Baba enjoy eating noodles like a child. For a brief moment, she drifted in her loving thoughts about Abhay when Baba finally asked, "Nusrat is so sweet. Then who was Hala Khan who had no hesitation and who never thought twice before firing a bullet at Abhay with an intent to kill him?"

With that question, the entire environment suddenly became sensitive, the clouds in the sky darker, and their conversation serious. That initiated the story of Nusrat Javed and she began to tell him the story, "Hala means glory, but that act on that ill-fated night added a dark chapter in my life, Baba. But I had to do that"

"Go on."

Happy Family was Ruined

Even before he barely said those two words, Nusrat began, "The story of Nusrat Javed becoming Hala Khan began four years before my birth. My Abbu, (Father) a government school teacher; Badi Ammi, (The first wife of her father), Aapa, (Elder Sister), and Rashid Bhai were happily settled in Noori village in Kashmir Valley. Noori is a true embodiment of Jannat (Heaven) on Earth. We were a happy family and we owned two houses, some land, and two large apple orchards there. Noori was a peaceful place and it was untouched by terrorism. My Aapa was pursuing medicines and she was doing her internship at AIIMS, New Delhi, and Rashid Bhai who was just 14 years old then was a budding cricketer at the junior national level."

She looked at Baba with sadness in her eyes and continued, "Then came that horrible day in our lives when the Security Forces conducted a cordon and search operation at Noori some 29 years ago. I don't know why, but two unscrupulous and evil men took turns to rape my Ammi and Aapa, brutalised them, and later killed them in cold blood. The Security Forces personnel carried their defiled bodies away and buried them in obscurity, thus denying the family an opportunity of arranging even a decent burial for them"

Nusrat was shaking in anger and she was crying. Baba was appalled, he was shaken too but he consoled her, and said, "I have understood everything, my child, I don't want you to continue any further. I am sorry for making you remember and relive that horror of your life."

She looked through him and said, "Baba, my story had its genesis there, but it began much later. I was not even born then."

Rashid Javed

Baba kept quiet and allowed her to continue, "My Abbu and Rashid Bhai were held hostage and they heard the painful shrieks of my Badi Ammi and Aapa. The helplessness in bearing those horrible atrocities on their loved ones had manifested differently for my Abbu and Bhai." She was crying continuously while narrating that inhuman incident, Baba felt guilty for making her bear those painful memories, and he urged her to stop once again. But she could not and continued, "My Abbu went numb in his pain, but my Bhai was angry. He was angrier at the media trial which dubbed our family as terrorists and supporters of LeT and destroyed the peace of Noori forever. Unable to bear the humiliation, Rashid Bhai stopped playing cricket, crossed over to the other side of the line of control, and was radicalised. He was very highly trained at the terrorist camps of Afghanistan, Iraq, and Pakistan. He was a tall and handsome man. He was very strong and folklores about him said that he was endowed with special powers by the Almighty Allah. No ordinary man could ever kill him. He had vowed to avenge the humiliation and killing of his mother and elder sister. But he never killed civilians or committed atrocities on them. He was like a local Robinhood who helped the needy and poor and stood by them in their times of despair. He kept terrorism at bay from Noori and allowed peace and prosperity to prevail there. With that kind of firm assurance, Noori once again became an economic hub of Kashmir Valley and the residents sent their children for education to the best of the cities in our country. But he killed Security Forces personnel at will and he soon became the most wanted terrorist for the Indian establishment. He used to say prophetically to me, "You shall marry the young man who could and would kill me." I dreaded the thought of losing him and prayed to Allah never to send such a man ever, even if I had to remain unmarried for life. But probably, Rashid Bhai knew that he was living on the edge and the bullets were stronger than the strongest."

The First Meeting

She paused for some moments, ordered another cup of tea for Baba, and then spoke further. She said, "After a few years, Abbu remarried my Ammi Aameena Akhtar in a simple ceremony, and I was born. When I was five years old, my Abbu was transferred to RIMC, Dehradun. There I met Abhay for the first time and for whatever reason I instantly liked him. He was in class VIII. He excelled both in academics and sports. He was very affectionate towards me. I remember an inter-house football match we saw together in RIMC because for the entire duration of that match I sat on his palm. His hand went numb, but he did not remove it from under me. It was crazy, but I guess children are like that only."

Baba was getting the connection between them and couldn't help but notice a shy smile descend on her pretty face, but he did not interrupt her flow as she went ahead, "I was very happy when he cleared the Union Public Service Commission Examination (UPSC) for his selection to NDA, Khadakwasla, Pune. A few years later, Abbu was transferred to Rahimabad, near Srinagar and I went to Saint Stephen's College and graduated in English Literature from DU (Delhi University). For all those years, I never forgot Abhay. Perhaps, he had put a chain through my heart that bound me to him permanently."

Her Brother was Killed

She paused for a moment and continued further, "I distinctly remember it was 05/09/2144 and I was getting married to Maulvi Shehzad Mukhtar on that day. The whole of Noori was beautifully decorated. I wore an expensive bridal dress. Rashid Bhai had come to be with me during my Nikah. However, Bhai's accomplice and a traitor Amanullah Pathan stabbed him in the back and gave a tip-off to the Army about him. He came to Noori with Bhai, but he slipped away during the Army operation instead of helping my brother and his buddies who had reposed so much trust in him. An Army team came in and surrounded our house stealthily. Rashid Bhai had just gone out to the balcony of our home when he was fired upon and the bullet pierced through his right shoulder. It was perhaps a coincidence that I could injure Abhay on his right shoulder only. Hearing the sound of the gunfire, I immediately reached out to Rashid Bhai and saw a glimpse of the Army man who fired the bullet before Rashid Bhai pushed me into the house and he jumped on him in order to draw the Army team away from our home and save every one of us. My would-be groom Shehzad was later killed in the crossfire. Soon we came to know that Rashid Bhai was killed by the Army officer who himself was grievously injured in a bloody fight with him. We were informed that the throat of my brother was slit and he had injuries all over on his body. The brutality of his killing was reminiscent of the brutality with which my Badi Ammi and Aapa were killed 29 years back. We were seething with anger, and as if to add insult to the injury, we were denied the right to give him a decent burial just like the way we were earlier denied that right for my Badi Ammi and Aapa. Fearing the glorification of his death, my brother's body was flown out by an Airforce Chopper to an undisclosed location and Army buried him too in anonymity."

While describing the gruesome killing of her brother, she sobbed uncontrollably, Baba tried to calm her down and said, "I can't hear anymore, let's go home."

"Please Baba, let me continue and finish it once and for all."

"I trust you Beta, I am sorry."

"I had to tell you all this someday or the other, please hear me out today. And why should you be sorry?"

Wanted Revenge

Baba reluctantly allowed her to complete her story. Even the incessant rains were not relenting, she picked up from where she had left and said, "I was a very delicate and timid girl, but the ruthless killing of Rashid Bhai emboldened me beyond belief. I wanted to avenge that killing. I had to kill the Army officer even at the cost of my life or whatever cost. My parents tried their best to dissuade me, even our community made a vain attempt to stop me from taking the drastic step, but I simply refused to listen. My love for Rashid Bhai would not settle for anything less than death for that butcher Army officer. Posterity would judge whether I was wrong or right but I certainly paid a huge cost.

"I crossed over to Pakistan's side of the line of control and I was radicalised in a Masjid in Pakistan-occupied Kashmir. From there, I was taken to a terrorist training camp where I was given basic training which included the firing of weapons and acquaintance with non-electronic methods of communications. Thereafter, I was moved to a field hospital where I was given preliminary training in intensive medical care. Upon completion of that training, I was given the name of Hala Khan, fake identity documents, and a fake medical training certificate from Breach Candy Hospital, Mumbai. I was informed that Mullah Akhbar alias Firoze Khan would be my handler, Ms. Hania Saeed and Sana Khan would be my backup, and they were the ones through whom my handler would communicate with me. The use of the mobile phone was strictly forbidden. I was given two vials of potassium cyanide and my entry to the Army Hospital Srinagar was facilitated through the hospital-approved agency which was appointed to provide additional nursing support to the Army Hospital. I was tasked to poison the killer Army officer while he was in the ICU. The task was easy and I was almost like a Fedayeen who had decided to die in the process of the completion of the assigned mission. It took me just ten days to win over the confidence of the sister-in-charge of the ICU. Unfortunately, I was not posted to the ICU and was instead assigned to the officers' ward. I wanted to poison him the very first day when I was supposed to meet him and I had conveyed the same to my handler who advised me to hold on till further instructions from him. I hated the man who killed my brother so brutally and as such, I was quite disappointed with those instructions from my handler. It was conveyed to me through Hania that I must first gain the confidence of the environment before the execution of my task.

She Won't Kill

Perhaps, Allah had wished that I don't kill him and when I saw Abhay for the first time after RIMC, I immediately recognised him, and something in my Antarman (Inner Realm) told me that I can't kill him. My resolve to spare his life got firmer when I checked and confirmed his name in his medical case file. I was quite convinced that he was the same Abhay whom I had met at the RIMC, Dehradun. That's the greatest dilemma that I had ever faced in my life, the dilemma between my love for my brother, my revenge, and my real feelings for his killer. Yes, my feelings were real, and I did not know why I was feeling for him the way I never felt for any other man in my life including Shehzad Mukhtar. There is no concept of rebirth in my faith, yet the feeling personified the encounters of souls where love if I could call that so then, triumphed over hatred. And that too for a man who killed my brother and whom I met for the first time thereafter. And yes, it rained heavily that day also and I was pushed into a Nimbus Cloud of Unknowing." It was time for them to go, but as they prepared to move, the intensity of the rains increased once again and they were forced to stay there. It appeared that even cloud and rain were listening to her story. She took a deep breath and said, "Finally after a fortnight or so, I had made a place for myself there and I got the clear orders to eliminate Abhay. I did not want to poison him and what was more surprising was that even Hania and Sana did not want me to kill him for whatever reason. They were good girls who paid the price of their goodness when I was in NIA's custody. Thereafter, I came to Mussoorie with Abhay and met all of you. My handler was very unhappy with me. Abhay and I were coming close, he expressed his feelings for me, but I could not reciprocate because the bitter battles were raging in my Antarman.

Parents Held Hostage

Quite interestingly, on that ill-fated day, we both sat at this very place, it was raining as much and Abhay shared the story of his life with me later that afternoon in his room. Everything was normal till then, but that evening around 5:00 p. m. I got an anonymous phone call that informed me of a handwritten note that had been delivered to my room and the caller asked me to read that note and destroy the same immediately thereafter. I rushed to my room and found a piece of paper wrapped around a stone lying on the balcony. That was a handwritten note that threatened me to kill Abhay that night itself, failing which my Ammi-Abbu, who were held hostage, would be killed. That note also informed me where you kept your pistol. The sound of the pistol fire was a signal to indicate the killing of Abhay, and for sparing the life of my parents. That was a very difficult choice for me. Believe me, Baba, I loved my parents much more than myself, but I could not ever think of killing Abhay for that. Having read the note, I went back to Abhay to hear the rest of the story of his life. Abhay is very sharp and he correctly read the kaleidoscopic expressions on my face and my body language which could not be normal. He knew that I was not listening to him anymore. I had no choice but to think fast and find a way to save my parents without causing any harm to him. Perhaps Allah guided me and it suddenly occurred to me that the requirement was only the sound of gunfire and as such there was no need to kill him. Though that was risky, I thought that was the best option in the given circumstances. That evening, I came to your room and took your pistol away. I usually never stayed in Abhay's room past 10:00 p. m. but that night I stayed with him till 11:00 p. m. As I prepared myself to fire the pistol, he went to the washroom. I had no intention whatsoever to hurt him, he came out of the washroom, saw me holding the pistol, and said, "What are you doing Khaani?" When I saw him, I got very nervous, my hands were shaking, and my mind was shuttling between my parents' lives and his life. I involuntarily spoke to myself, "Allah please, I am sorry, I don't want to, I can't, but I have to do this." My feelings nauseated me and I just did not want to think. I just wanted that ordeal to be over, I closed my eyes and fired the pistol. Abhay wanted to kill my brother, but he missed his aim; I wanted him to live, so I deliberately missed my aim. Perhaps, he took evasive action, and the bullet I aimed nowhere found his right shoulder perhaps at the same spot where his bullet had injured my brother. That was the most unfortunate moment of my life from where it took a sharp turn into my worst nightmare.

Her Revenge Found Her Love

My sufferings began the moment I left your beautiful home. I received the first slap in 20 years of my life that night and that marked the beginning of the humiliation that went beyond every figment of my imagination. I was broken physically, emotionally, mentally, and psychologically. Some of those humans crossed all the limits of human depravity. Although I did not break, they scarred both my mind and body to a great extent. But you know what Baba, Allah helped me there also. He punished me, and when his punishment was over, He numbed my senses and my feeling and kept them with him, and returned them to me only when I saw Abhay at the NIA court. That helped me bear all my pains with remarkable courage. I committed the crime but my biggest mistake was that I did not accept the killing of my brother as Allah's wish. The decision to take revenge ruined my life. I became an object, a toy, in the hands of the terrorists and various instruments of the state. Beyond hurting Abhay against my wish and playing a puppet in the hands of terrorists, I was innocent. Whatever I knew, I told both the police and NIA and I did not know more than that. It was a sort of double whammy that NIA thought I was hiding the facts from them, and the terror outfit thought I was a threat to them and they held my elderly parents hostage to enforce silence on me. The fact of the matter was that I knew no more than what I had narrated to the investigating agencies. The system had to teach me harshly what it took to hurt an Army guy. Perhaps, I was destined to take revenge because that became the reason for finding my love. Thereafter, she went on to tell him about the arduous journey of her life after her release from the Tihar Jail back to Mussoorie.

In Her Suffering She Found Her

Baba had heard her patiently, but he wondered how could that young woman endure so much indignity in her life. He was quite disturbed when he said, "Your Allah was unfair to you."

"Why do you say that Baba?"

"He gave you so much suffering."

"Baba Allah introduced me to myself in my sufferings."

"How?"

She said, "In the midst of hate, I found there was, within me, an invincible love. In the midst of tears, I found there was, an invincible smile. In the midst of chaos, I found there was, an invincible calm. I realised, through it all, that in the midst of winter, I found there was, within me, an invincible summer. And that makes me happy. For it says that no matter how hard the world pushes against me, within me, there's something stronger, something better, pushing right back."

Pure Love

Thereafter, Abhay came back into my life and his false testimony in the NIA court ended my agony to a great extent and ignited my latent love for him. It was never gratitude; it was pure love. He does not even know that I love him, and I will never tell him that I love him. I want him to feel the way I feel his love. It was Allah's intervention and yet another coincidence that Abhay removed both my suitors from our way. He killed my would-be husband on the day of my Nikah, and Amanullah Pathan on the day he was abducting me for Nikah. Coincidence is God's way of remaining anonymous. Allah surely ordained our union and He could not allow anyone to come between us. When they were walking back home, she thought that it was Allah's blessing that paved the way for her possible union with someone she loved and who loved her more than himself. She asked herself, "How did Rashid Bhai know that? Was he a messenger of Allah? They were destined to meet. Baba too remained quiet, but he had decided that he would be blessed to have Nusrat Javed as his daughter-in-law. And he was so excited that he shared his thoughts with Nalini, Naveli, and Abhay on the same very day. Thakuraien Sahiba's home was finally finding the lasting happiness that was long overdue, and for sure it deserved it all the way.

REUNION OF SOULS

Someday, everything will make perfect sense, so for now, laugh at the confusion, smile through the tears, and keep reminding yourself that everything happens for a reason.

Abhay Proposed

Later that night, Abhay called her and proposed to her. She had no words except to thank Allah for his blessings. Both of them were in the seventh heaven of happiness. Abhay asked,

"Do you love me?

She smiled and said, "I don't know."

"What do you mean you don't know?"

"I mean I don't know."

Abhay knew she was being naughty and he asked, "Okay will you miss me?"

She was enjoying teasing him and said, "No."

"What do you mean no?"

"No means no."

That conversation between the lovers lingered on till the time battery of her phone was exhausted.

Her Feelings

Her excitement did not allow her to sleep that night. She thanked Allah many times. Before she slept, she thought of their intimate conversation of that night. She said to herself, "Main Miss Karoongi? Miss Toh Shayad Ek Chota Lafz Hai Na Us Sasaad Ke Liye Jo Main Rakhne Lagi Hun Tumhaare Liye. Aur Aab Main Apne Aap Se Darne Lagi Hun. Kisi Se Mohabbat Insaan Ko Bahot Kamzore Kar Deti Hai. Bahot Bebas, Mazboor, Mehkoom Aur Mujhe Inn Teeno Cheezon Se Nafrat Hai. Lekin Uske Bawzood Tum Meri Zindagi Ka Markaz Bante Ja Rahe Ho. Tum Mujh Se Poochte Ho Ke Mujhe Tumhaari Kya Baat Acchie Lagti Hai. Main Tumhe Ye Kaise Kahoon Ki Mujhe Tumhaari Kon Si Baat Acchie Nahin Lagti. Apne Irdgird Tumhaara Ghoomna, Mere Wazood Se Na Hatne Wali Tumhaari Gehrie Bolti Nazaren, Tumhaari Har Waqt Ki Tawwazoo, Tumhaara Jaan Chidakne Wala Har Andaaz. Har Baar Jab Tum Mere Liye Aitraaman Khade Hote Ho Toh Mein Tumhaare Saamne Jhookne Lagti Hun. Aur Kya Kuch Nahin Jo Mujhe Tumhaare Saamne Moem Nahin Karta. Par Ye Sab Main Tumko Khabhie Nahi Bataoongie. Tumhare Har Wade Par Hasungie, Tumhaari Har Baat Ka Mazaak Udaungie. Tum Mujhe Sangemarmar Samajhte Ho Toh Samajhte Raho, Mein Tumhaare Saamne Ret Ki Deewar Nahin Ban Sakti, Mujhe Toot Jane Se Khauff Aata Hai."

(Will I miss you? Missing is perhaps a small word as compared to what I feel for you, and I am getting scared of myself now. Love makes you very weak, helpless, dependent, and lonely, and I hate these things in my life. But, despite this, you are becoming the reference point of my life. You often ask me what I like about you. How do I tell you there is nothing that I dislike about you? I feel your presence around me all the time, your deep expressive eyes, your naughtiness, and your attitude of love, I love everything about you. When you stand up in respect for me, I want to bow down before you in reverence for you. Your love melts me. But I will never tell you all this, I will laugh your promises off, and I will laugh at everything you say. You feel I am like a marble who has no emotions, be it so? I can't become a wall of sand because I am afraid of breaking my heart and hurting my feelings.)

She smiled and slept with those naughty thoughts.

Wedding Plans

Soon the wedding dates were fixed and preparations began in the right earnest. Nalini and Naveli came in full strength. Baba wanted that the wedding to be solemnised in both Muslim and Hindu traditions. Abhay did not believe in rituals, but he gave in to his Baba's wishes. The plan that fanned out was that the Nikah would be at the ancestral home of Nusrat at Noori, followed by the wedding as per the Hindu customs at Triyuginarayan, and a grand reception at Mussoorie. Plans having been firmed up; the hectic preparations began at all the venues. As the wedding dates approached nearer, their home was lit up, celebrations began and a bonanza of fun and frolic unfolded in every nook and corner of their home. There was music in the air and song in every heart. Nikah was at Noori and accordingly, Nusrat moved to Noori two days before the date of Nikah.

Nikah

Noori village was decked up for the Nikah of their daughter. Her house was very tastefully decorated with flowers as per Muslim traditions. Nusrat's relatives and friends made affectionate arrangements for the reception of the Baraat (Wedding Procession). Nature was in its full bloom and expressed its joys in the salubrious climate and all the colours of different varieties of flowers. In fact, everyone was awestruck by the natural beauty of Noori. That was an out-of-the-world serene landscape tucked up in the lap of mighty Himalayas, bestowed with picturesque locale and inexorable beauty. The beauty found an all-new meaning when they entered that paradise of tranquillity. The serene ambience and salubrious climate welcomed them in Noori and they almost felt that the place had cast a magic spell upon them to replenish their soul and rejuvenate their entire beingness. Seeing the vivid green of grass and shrubs, Baba found himself feeling overjoyed in admiration of that distinct shade of green that was so natural. In witnessing the magnificence of nature, he renewed his heart and soul by naturally unveiling a spirit of awe and reverence in him. Baba realised that when it came to such beauty of Nature, time stopped, the space became silent and the soul fell asleep while he was awake. There was a kind of quiet mystery about that good place that made everyone very happy. But Abhay's eyes were searching to steal a glimpse of Nusrat. His senses came alive when she gave a glimpse of her on the same balcony where he saw her for the first time some six years ago. He realised that the beautiful girl he saw in his dreams was indeed Nusrat. He couldn't help slipping briefly into the cloud of unknowing. He felt that their union was blessed by the desire of the divinity, and in a mystic experience, he heard the same voice that he had heard before, speak to him and that clearly said, "I have fulfilled my promise. Saral shall meet you again, you won't recognise each other, but the eternal bond will blossom into a love for both of you. Remember, memories are barred from crossing the light cones, but there are no such bars on the bonds of souls." Abhay knew that he had had such a conversation before and heard the same voice in one of his dreams as well. The divine voice had clearly established the past life connection between Nusrat and him. Before he could be lost in those mystic thoughts, she showed up on the balcony once again. She was wearing a white saree with a green border; her hairs were open and she was beautiful; the special kind of beauty that you cannot unsee, the kind which remains etched in your heart for a long time. She was an epitome of that precise beauty to the extent that calling her beautiful was an understatement. She had an aura around her. Everything about her had its own charm and that was arousing Abhay's impatience to go nearer to her. He was a bit shaken by the mystic experience, a bit shy too, he was rather uncomfortable with the overflow of his feelings; and it was at that precious moment, that she gestured him to come to her, laughed, and ran inside. Abhay smiled and he felt that he had seen some woman in the past she was also wearing a white saree with a green border, and her hairs were open, and she was beautiful. That memory just flashed in his mind and went away as quickly as it came. He could not remember anything more than that and he dumped that feeling for good.

The wedding was solemnised with traditional Muslim fervour followed by a feat of exotic Kashmiri dishes. After the Nikah, all of them went to Srinagar and stayed the night there.

Noori Beckoned Abhay

All of them were sitting together and praising the beauty of Noori that night when Naveli asked Abhay, "Bhai (Brother), who is more beautiful, Noori or Nusrat Bhabhi (Sister-in-Law)?

Everyone laughed, Abhay just smiled and pointed towards Nusrat. Nusrat gave a shy smile as Nalini joined that interesting conversation and asked, "Bhai, what attracted you to Noori?

Abhay thought for a while and he remembered that he always wanted to go to Noori but could not assign any reason for that. He saw everyone waiting for his answer, he kept quiet and once again pointed towards Nusrat.

This time Nusrat was somewhat serious when she said, "Tell the truth, Abhay?"

He replied, "This is the truth, Nusrat. I actually did not know why I went to Noori. Probably my destiny took me there for a glimpse of you on your balcony and tied me to you forever."

Marriage at Triyuginarayan

The next day they flew to Dehradun and after a day's rest, they took Pawan Hans helicopters to Triyuginarayan for their nuptials to be solemnised in a spiritual ambience. Triyuginarayan Temple is nestled in Uttarakhand's Triyuginarayan village and it is believed that Lord Shiva got married to the daughter of

Himavat, Goddess Parvati at this venue. The celestial wedding was witnessed by Lord Vishnu. A perpetual flame burns in front of the temple, which is believed to have been burning since the time of the marriage of Mahadev and Devi Parvati about three eons or Yuga ago. Hence, the name, Triyuginarayan with Tri meaning three, Yugi meaning Epochs, and Narayan as a synonym for Lord Vishnu. When the Pheras (The 7 Hindu Wedding Vows) began, Abhay had a flash of memories where he was taking Pheras with Nusrat, but they were not wearing the traditional wedding dresses. Was she Nusrat or Saral? He definitely felt the past life connection. He did not want to believe that, but he was seeing themselves getting married there earlier also. But, why weren't they dressed as bride and groom? After the wedding ceremony, all of them stayed the night there and the next day, they flew back to Dehradun for a grand reception at Mussoorie. The grand reception was followed by the post-wedding rituals and celebrations over the next few days. Although sufficient leisure time was integral to the wedding plan, pleasure exhausted all of them as it always did and with a view to letting happiness sink in, the next couple of days were used by everyone for rest, refit, and reorganisation. Soon the day arrived when Nalini, Naveli, and all family members departed leaving Baba alone with Nusrat and Abhay. The wedding events kept them so busy that Nusrat and Abhay could hardly have any time to themselves.

Rahul and Saral

*But everything that once lived, lives on forever. In the
eternity of time.*

Nusrat and Abhay

When finally, they were together, Abhay saw her, his eyes got
glued to her divine face and he was dumbstruck in awe of
her sensuality. Those were very awkward moments, she was
smiling, and Abhay was embarrassingly feeling shy, he had
to make an effort to take his eyes off her face but still, he
remained quite fidgety. The most beautiful smile illuminated
her face when he unwittingly blurted out, "Who are you?" and
she replied very naturally looking into his eyes, "I am Saral".
Perhaps she did not realise what she had said, but Abhay was
quite sure that they had met in the past life cone as Rahul and
Saral. That was a déjà vu moment for him and he felt blessed.
As if guided by some divine intervention, suddenly the
weather took a turn and it started raining heavily. The reunion
of Nusrat and Abhay was solemnised and blessed by cloud
and rain. Their lovemaking was tender and thereafter they
together had some fruits and herbs, and both felt energetic,

fulfilled, and happy. As they began to discover each other better with time, they shared some scintillating conversations between them during the days and fabulous lovemaking on those beautiful nights that followed and the bliss continued whenever they were together. Her conversational skills and knowledge of the anatomy of "Humaning" (The word is not found in any dictionary and yet it made sense) were simply superb. Abhay just glided in the flow and flair of his feelings. He revealed every facet of his life to her with utmost honesty, and she had become the centre focus of his life. She loved everything about him, but she deliberately held herself back and did not quite express that much. She was perhaps scared of love or maybe quite protective about her newly discovered happiness. Abhay took life as it came and with time fell deeply in love with her. Nusrat was completing him in every sense of the word and he was finding the hither-to-unknown meaning of life in her company. He was enriched, wore the glow of her company, and felt blessed. She perhaps possessed some special powers or was it the purity of her love that cleansed his perceptions on life and he met the perfection of his imperfections. He was willing to do anything for her, but all that she asked for was love, and Abhay did not disappoint her on that count ever. She made him feel like a king. Abhay had the most incredible sex with Nusrat. Their lovemaking was tender and tantalisingly slow; pleasure peaked and its potency percolated down to every pore of their entire beingness. Abhay had slept with many women, but sex with Nusrat was the most enriching and satisfying experience for him. He shared his feelings with her many times in those post-coital lazy moments. In one of those moments, she told him that it was love that made all the difference. And that gave him a chance to ask his favourite question, "Do you love me?"

Love

She smiled and asked him, "Do you know what is love? As he stared at her with his naughty inquisitiveness, she elaborated, "Love is the purest manifestation of all human emotions, it is the peak, the ultimate high, the essence of our emotional core".

"But emotions have no logic", Abhay said.

Nusrat looked at him for some time, smiled, and said, "Love has a delicate disposition and it also cannot bear the burden of logic".

Abhay was enjoying the conversation and teasingly he asked, "How can the love between Baba and me be the same as the love between you and me?"

She replied, "Love is love and nothing else. In its most common classical interpretation, love refers to the irresistible desire to obtain possession of the beloved, expressing a deficiency that the lover must remedy to reach perfection. Like the perfections of the soul and the body, love thus admits hierarchical horizons. However, its underlying reality is the aspiration to the beauty which God Almighty had manifested in the world when he created humans in his own image. Simply put, experiencing love is understanding love."

"Do you love me?"

"I am sleepy."

"Do you love me?"

She gave a lazy smile and before she dozed off, she said, "No, I am scared of love."

The Honeymoon

Nusrat was a beautiful and disciplined woman who had come to become central to Abhay's life. She was a woman of substance who cared for and loved him with radical honesty and sincerity. Abhay was very impressed by her simplicity, eloquence, her knowledge of the Urdu language, wit and humour, and of course her superb rapport with Baba. Nusrat and Baba were best friends. Their home became livelier, the garden greener, she cared for everyone on their staff, and they loved her. Abhay and Nusrat became inseparable and that established a beautiful Raabta between them. After about a fortnight after their wedding, they were enjoying their breakfast when Baba gifted them air tickets for a fortnight-long trip to Europe and US. Baba had very meticulously planned the itinerary for them, and that came naturally to him because he had included all the places where he had lived some of the most fabulous moments of his life with Sangeeta, and where they found their love for each other during their honeymoon some six decades ago. While planning that exact trip for them, he relived some of the best times he had in his life with his wife. As per the plan, Nusrat and Abhay flew to Paris, the city of love. Their love blossomed in full bloom and the Eiffel Tower, Notre Dame Cathedral, Louvre Museum, Champs Elysees, Cruise on the Seine, Moulin Rouge and Disneyland in the city of love became a witness and bore testimony to their whirlwind romance. The ensuing days saw them travel through the whole of Europe, Scandinavian countries, Los Angeles, Great Canyons, Las Vegas and Mammoth Lakes.

Nusrat Felt the Connect

In Mammoth Mountain there was a cosily tucked in place, naturally formed by rocks, where Nusrat and Abhay posed for a photo. As they stood there, the fellow travellers wholeheartedly applauded them for it was believed that any couple that stood there was deemed to have married there and then. Yet again, a memory flashed through his mind and he saw himself standing there with her. But they were not wearing the same clothes that they were wearing now. He was quite puzzled and his face bore a strange look. Nusrat noticed that and asked unexpectedly, "Have we been to this place earlier also? But this is the first time that I am here."

"Why do you say that?"

"A memory just flashed through my mind and I saw myself standing with you here. But there you were wearing the First Gorkha Rifles Cap, not the Balidaan (Sacrifice) Cap you are wearing now."

"It is indeed strange because I saw the same memory flash through my mind too. Are we made for each other for ages?"

That experience became the most defining moment of their lives. Something changed forever in their Antarman that made it Atarangee forever. They did talk about it for a long time, but they could not understand anything. They became closer to each other and hoped for more clarity in times to come. The night at "The Village" was the most romantic night of their lives together. That night they became one once again, made love slowly, savouring the bliss and give of every single moment. That was the most happening night of their life when they professed their deep love for each other, and she finally admitted that she loved him more than she loved herself. He was her first love and her feelings for him were very intense. She felt that they had made love there earlier also.

A few years later they were blessed with twin daughters. Baba named them Mishmi and Neetisha.

Their Souls are Identical

*"You enter a dream for the heck of it; And know not the
way to exit route;*

*From the world you brought alive; In sleep, awake to
desires manifest;*

*In the raging flame that consumes; Your being stranded
amidst embers:*

*Aglow, each spark ignites your mind; Where the forest
green will grow anew;*

*Once upon a time in the future past; Luring the hunter
once more;*

In pursuit of the game, you love."

— The dreamer

Brave Drop meets the Ocean

Ehad, who was quietly listening to the conversation between
Awargi and Sajda regarding SMOTH of "Smile and Tear",
finally broke her long silence and said, "Since Saral is the Smile
for him, I will certainly ensure that she illuminates Rahul's face
at an appropriate juncture."

"But where is she now?", asked Sajda."

"She is a brave drop of water who had met the ocean and has since returned to her Nimbus Cloud for her love belongs there; Picture this: "Nusrat is gazing at the little stream in front of her. It seems to be dancing as it tumbled over little rocks and stones on its way. It never gets tired of flowing. It is not flowing because someone asked it to, but because it is in its nature. Though separate, this stream belongs to the ocean. Every drop flowing in it had emerged from the ocean and would eventually return to it. And along its journey, it becomes the reason for many flowers blossoming, many birds quenching their thirst, many hearts rejoicing in its beauty, many colourful fish swimming … it is the longing of the stream to merge into the ocean that makes it flow. Love is the basis of its existence. And between the longing and the love, life flourishes". Ehad replied and further said – "When a drop feels connected to the ocean, it feels the strength of the ocean. This is subtle strength. The strength in a mind that feels connected to creation, the strength in a mind that is in the present moment, which is the field of all possibilities."

Sajda wondered and she said, "You said that earlier also."

"Yes, I had spoken this in the last-to-last light cone of Rahul when Saral had met the ocean and he was feeling miserable. In this case, this is for and about Nusrat."

"I mean you have said the same thing to Abhay in his dream."

Time has Limitations

"I have no control whatsoever over the communications within dreams. I don't even know if he heard a similar conversation in his dream. Awargi is the subtle element of his Antarman, and she may tell you better about that."

Awargi butted in and said, "Yes, he heard the similar conversation amongst us in his dream, but that was about his last-to-last light cone when they were Rahul and Saral and he had understood nothing of that." She paused for a moment and as if she remembered something, she asked, "Does Nusrat know she is Saral?" And she replied herself, "I feel even if she knows, it will at best only be imagination or a feeling and nothing more than that for her. That feeling will be true but not far from the truth. This is knowing by not knowing."

Ehad further explained, "Fortunately, or unfortunately, all three of us out here are the functions of creation and we are only the facilitators of life. Awargi is happiness, Sajda is prayer, And I am time. While both of you make life worth living, I am only a witness. I am not capable of imagination; in fact, I am not allowed access to it. Nobody knows life because it is mandated that way by the God Almighty. But He has created the six components that connect life and called them Dililah which is a word for the higher horizon. The word "Dililah" when expanded names these components as dreams, imagination, longing, intuitions, love, and hope. Life is all about them and nothing else. This is what I have witnessed. But I don't have any access to them. I also have no access to the communication of the Creator to the creation, matters of souls, and anything that is beyond the bounds of the universe."

"Can Nusrat and Abhay ever know that they were Saral and Rahul in their past life cone and that they are one and the same?"

"No, however, since life is connected, they feel that they have had a past life connection. There have been enough indications for them to feel the unbroken bonds of their love from their past lives. That everything's repeating; That this has all happened before like a massive déjà vu. But Saral and Rahul would never know that they have come together once again as Nusrat and Abhay. That's the law of Nature."

"That's unfair."

"No, that's very fair. Yesterday, today, and tomorrow are not consecutive, they are connected in a never-ending cycle. Everything is connected. Now imagine if the man had the capability to know his past, he could be in a situation in his present life where he would say to himself, "Her husband, who's fucking my mom, is looking for his son, who's my father." And that's complicated."

They Married Only Once

"Okay, so they have married twice."

"I can't tell you whether they have married twice or many times. However, whenever they both married each other, they would only be married once."

"Why would that be?"

"That would be so because their souls are identical. And do you know that Nature is polygamous in nature? Contrary to the societal mandate of monogamy, Nature is all about polygamy."

"Explain."

"I gave you that crude example of that just a few minutes back. Now that is polygamy. Take the case of Rahul and Saral.

They married each other only twice in their past four lives, including their present life. Their souls married only once with each other, but their bodies married many times to each other and even others; And many times, they remained single also. If I scan their recent lives, I find that Saral as Iqra was married to Haider, Rahul as Shakti had married Anjali Singh; Saral as Sneha was married to Ratan, and Rahul as Param was married to Sharda. Perhaps, their souls are destined to unite every alternate life. There is another interesting coincidence. When Iqra came into Shakti's thoughts when he was dying, they came together in their next life as Saral and Rahul; and when Sneha came into Param's thoughts when he was dying, they married each other as Nusrat and Abhay."

"That's very complicated."

Badal and Varsha

"No that's not. Life is only a function of the soul; the body is only a change of dress that the soul wears as per her choice. Lovers don't finally meet somewhere. They're in each other all along. That's because love is a subject of the soul, the totality of love is when the soul witnesses love, and laughs uncontrollably. See, Rahul and Saral are just names so are the names of every couple. The soul experiences whatever she has to and her choice of couples, as humans understand, is purely incidental. But the repeated meetings of the identical souls have an element of God in them and it is coincidental. Names are immaterial because souls are experiencing love through the bodies. To that extent, every couple is Rahul and Saral, and past or future life connections are only a feeling, a true feeling not far from the truth but there is no proof of that. That's a man-woman thing. In that sense, mythology defines every couple as Cloud and Rain, that is, Badal and Varsha."

"What is life?"

"Life is, love and work; work and love; that's all there is."

"What about the man?"

"Man is destined to fluctuate between his desires and pains."

"Elaborate."

"Man is a strange creature. All his actions are motivated by desire, his character forged by pain. As much as he may try to suppress that pain, to repress the desire, he cannot free himself from the eternal servitude to his feelings. For as long as the storm rages within him, he cannot find peace. Not in life; Not in death. And so, he will do what he must, day in, day out. The pain is his vessel, and desire is his compass. It is all that man is capable of.

That's the game, God loves. God is a naughty Guy!!!